Chapt...

Although it was over tw...
January 1988 still seems like it was only yesterday. This was the day that transformed the rest of my life, when I joined the Royal Electrical and Mechanical Engineers.

The train journey from Newcastle down to Wokingham was a long forlorn venture, but I was met at the train station by some people who I would get to know on quite a close intensity. I remember leaving the train, walking along the platform and through the small ticket office dragging my suitcase behind me. As I left the station I noticed the rain bouncing off the cobbled road in front of me, and the only shelter was an old corrugated iron bike shed at the far end of the car park, which seemed to be already bursting at the seams with young lads and their suitcases. I assumed they were heading my way, so I clattered my suitcase across the cobbled car park and squeezed myself through the bodies and musty cigarette smoke into a corner of the bike shed. Some of the lads looked at me with a nervous smile, and that's what confirmed for me that they were also heading to Arborfield for basic military training.

The fourteen weeks of basic training was arduous, but before I knew it I was at my passing out parade and going home for leave before going back to start my trade training as an armourer. It was good to see my friends when I got home, and we spent most of the two weeks partying and making the most of my time home.

Being in the army was a novelty in my town, so I soon became popular with the girls, which in turn made me quite ostracised with the local lads. On a number of occasions I got myself into a few scrapes with jealous ex boyfriends, but that was all part of the thrill.

On completion of my trade training, and after another few weeks leave, I was posted to an armoured infantry regiment in

Paderborn, Germany. During my four years here, I saw action in Northern Ireland and Bosnia, but also took part in military exercises in Poland and Canada. Although our operational tour of Northern Ireland was during an apparent "cease fire" period, we saw more action
in two months than what the previous regiment had experienced throughout their whole tour. Within weeks of arriving there, our camp had been petrol bombed twice, and about a month into the tour, one of our infantry soldiers had been shot during a street patrol. The sniper must've used a large calibre weapon as he had blown a hole through his chest which was big enough to fit my fist in, and the exit wound in his back was just a vast obliterated mess. He died instantly.

      On the second of August 1990, Saddam Hussein invaded Kuwait, and although we were itching to join the coalition out in Iraq, our regiment were not selected as we had not long returned from Northern Ireland. But thanks to the disintegration of Yugoslavia and a number of civil wars, we were soon to experience something totally distinctive in Bosnia. As part of an international peacekeeping contingency, the United Nations sent us into Bosnia where we spent a sustained emotional six months in a war torn town know as Gornji Vakuf. The UN may as well have sent us in with our hands tied behind our backs and without any weapons as we were so restricted as to the amount of force we were permitted to use. The precipitous area surrounding our camp was a haven for snipers who would often take pot luck shots at us while we were getting on with our day-to-day-business. Even I was shot at a few times whilst inspecting our vehicles' weaponry, but I was lucky enough to have never been hit. I could handle being in a sniper's line of sight, but what did cause me torment was when locals came to our front gate carrying a child. More often than not, the child had previously been playing in the fields with their friends and had come across a landmine, blowing off a leg or two in the process. The majority of these children did not survive, and it was us who these locals turned to for support. How is it possible to console a grieving parent when they are holding onto a lifeless child, saturated in blood and barely recognisable by their own family? Those children who were lucky enough to survive the atrocities of the land mines and ethnic cleansing spent most of their time begging for food and water.

The only positive outcome of my UN tour of Bosnia was the fact that I was promoted to Lance Corporal, but because of our situation, I wasn't able to celebrate in style- no alcohol.

Approximately two months after returning from Bosnia I received a posting order which sent me to a logistics regiment in Bielefeld, Germany. Apart from the occasional drunken brawl with the Germans in town, the three years I spent with this regiment were quite uneventful. This gave me the opportunity to concentrate on my career more and attend some courses which helped me gain promotion to Corporal. As well as sticking to my trade, I also became a physical training instructor and took the opportunity to excel in the sports I enjoy. The regimental gym became my second home and I soon became a prominent member of the regimental boxing team. After several successful fights in the inter squadron competitions, I was chosen to fight for the army team.

My career as an army boxer was short lived when the team made a visit to Portsmouth for a competition against the navy. On the night before my fight, we were all generously invited to the officers' mess, and it wasn't long before the quiet social event erupted into a drunken brawl. One of the navy boxers made remarks about the stereo typed mentality of the army, and unfortunately for him, I did not agree with him. The majority of the fight in the mess was a blur, and after waking up in one of the guardroom cells the next morning, I knew I was neck deep in shit. I remained under close arrest for the duration of the team's visit, and when I returned to my unit I was charged for being drunk and disorderly, and assault. I was fined four hundred and fifty pounds, and reduced to the rank of lance corporal. The Chelsea Pensioners were in for a good Christmas that year.

My reputation as a soldier and a tradesman diminished slightly, and this was reflected in my annual reports. But my popularity amongst the junior ranks had rocketed, and I soon came across as a bit of a hard case and a "jack-the-lad". It was at this point when I realised I was in need of a reality check and decided to give myself a fresh start. I applied for a new posting and was sent to another logistics regiment in Gutersloh, Germany. My reputation
followed me to my new regiment, but I strived to improve myself by concentrating on my work and my fitness. Due to my little incident in Portsmouth, I was no longer allowed to box, but as a physical training instructor I helped to train the regimental team. I also helped to run and organise a few major athletics meetings. My hard work soon paid off and within a year of being at the unit I was promoted back to corporal.

The highlight of being with this regiment was the five months I spent in Oman on an operational exercise. We were based in the port of Salalah, and we set up our own little home comforts, including a bar. Some of our weekends were free so we were permitted to visit the town centre where we would buy cheap gold or maybe even visit the small barber shop for an old fashioned "cut throat" shave. Occasionally, on a Sunday we would travel to the Hilton hotel where we would lounge by the pool, play volleyball on the beach or lie in the menthol sauna before having a relaxing full body massage.

One particular evening, I and three of my colleagues had just finished a shopping spree in town, so we flagged down a taxi to take us back to the port where our camp was. A yellow cab pulled over and we got into it. My guts churned as I looked at the taxi driver and noticed that he had only one eye, his left hand had been amputated, and the "trigger" finger of his right hand was missing. This instantly told me he wasn't the type of man you can

trust. It also crossed my mind how the hell he managed to drive a car. Unfortunately, by the time this had all sunk in, the taxi was moving, so we couldn't exactly leave without making a scene. I told the taxi driver that we wanted to head for Salalah port, but he asked us if we wanted to go somewhere where there were "naughty" ladies. He grinned while he said this, and I noticed he also had only one tooth which was on the verge of rotting away. I thanked him for the offer, but declined, asking him again to take us to the port. As the taxi approached a small roundabout, the driver took the first exit, rather than the usual second exit towards the port. This was leading us into a part of town we were not familiar with, and I asked the driver to turn around and go the usual route. He looked at me and
started to laugh hysterically saying that he insisted on us visiting these "ladies". Before he could take us even deeper into unfamiliar territory, I decided to act, quickly. Whilst the other three were starting to panic on the back seat, I yanked with both hands on the handbrake until the car came to a skidding halt in the middle of the dusty road and stalled. I had pulled so hard on the lever I felt the handbrake cable snap. Before the driver had the opportunity to react, I punched him square on the chin, knocking him out, and he slumped over the steering wheel. I told the lads to get out the car, and as I left I pulled the car keys out of the ignition and grabbed the driver identity badge which was hanging on his rear view mirror. The four of us sprinted back up to the roundabout and back into town. I found a pay phone and contacted the military police to come and get us, as I wasn't entirely comfortable about getting into another taxi. Because of that incident, the whole regiment were barred from going into town for safety reasons.

My time with the logistics regiment had come to a sad end, and I was moved on to an armoured reconnaissance regiment in Catterick, North Yorkshire. The majority of my time with these was spent on exercise and firing camps, but this kept me busy as the C.V.R.T's (Combat Vehicle Reconnaissance Tracked) they used were very outdated so I always had plenty of work to do. The firing camps were my busiest times as I had to carry out pre firing checks every morning, then spend the rest of the days repairing any damaged weaponry. Although we were never sent on any operational tours during my time with the cavalry, we were always kept busy.

Being posted to Catterick gave me the opportunity to spend most of my free weekends at home in Sunderland, as it was less than an hour away. It felt good being able to catch up with my old friends, and being part of my life again. Although I never regretted joining the army, I sometimes realised what I had missed out on over the years, and I made the most of being with them again. It was then when I met up with an old school sweetheart, Sandra. I hadn't seen her since I was seventeen, yet she had never changed or aged at all. Still beautiful, just as I remember. We hit it off straight away,
and we spent most of our weekends together. As things became more serious, I began inviting her to social functions at our corporals' mess and I could see that she was enjoying this lifestyle. She was proud of her boyfriend being part of something so important, and relished in letting her friends know that she was with a "hero". Eighteen months from us getting together, she told me that she was expecting our baby, and I was overjoyed. Being the typical old fashioned man, I wanted to do things correctly and make our life complete, and asked Sandra to marry me before the baby was born.

The wedding was a private affair where we invited close family and a few friends to the ceremony at Sunderland Civic Centre, then held a small function in the private room of our favourite pub on the sea front. We spent a week in Tenerife for our honeymoon, and four months later our little boy, Cameron, was born. Sandra and Cameron moved down to Catterick with me and our life was happy.

After four years with the cavalry, I was promoted to sergeant which meant another posting. I and the family moved back over to Germany where I started work with an armoured medical regiment. My main job here was to look after the regiment's armoury of SA80's and Browning pistols, but I was also responsible for assisting with the regimental fitness programme. Me, Sandra and Cameron moved into a little house in Munster, and when Cameron started kindergarten, Sandra got herself a part time job in the officer's mess as a waitress. So as far as I was concerned, life couldn't be better.

Chapter 2

The opening of 2003 was interesting as the situation heated up in Iraq over the issue of weapons of mass destruction, and within weeks rumours were flying that we were heading out there to support a field hospital.

On the morning of Saturday the eighth of February 2003, I kissed my wife and son goodbye and made my way to the barracks to prepare for my flight to Basra airport. We were taken by coach to Hannover airport, where we flew to RAF Brize Norton, and then we were flown by Hercules into Basra. Our advance party had already been in Basra for a few days and had already set up the field hospital ready to take casualties if or when anything broke out.

I'd only been at the airport for a few hours when a panic stricken voice came over the PA system shouting, "gas, gas, gas!" This was my cue to don my respirator and NBC suit. The temperature was already ridiculously high, but the heat became even more intense once I was inside my charcoal lined suit and rubber boots and gloves and respirator. I could feel the mouth piece of my respirator slowly filling up with sweat, but I knew this was no drill, so it wasn't coming off my face, despite the severe discomfort. An hour or so later, we were given the "all clear", so I stripped back down to my combat trousers and t shirt, poured the sweat out of my respirator and packed away my NBC equipment ready for the next time. The following few weeks consisted of similar situations, and sometimes we were rudely awoken during the night because of the threat of a chemical attack.

On the eighteenth of March 2003, the Americans announced that they were giving Saddam Hussein fort eight hours to move out of Iraq because they were about to attack. Two days later, at approximately 0615hrs, the Americans fired their missiles into Baghdad, he war had started. Another two days later, we heard news that over eight thousand Iraqi soldiers surrendered in the South and welcomed the coalition forces with open arms. So much for the "mother of all wars".

The majority of the casualties received into our field hospital were Iraqi soldiers and civilians. Our soldiers were being admitted for heat injuries and the occasional gun shot wound. The war was short lived, but we remained for another two months or so continuing to take in casualties. By the end of the tour, I was an expert with masking and unmasking drills. As our time was drawing to a close, a huge contingency of Territorial Army soldiers were sent to us, which lightened our work load immensely, and gave us a little time to relax more before returning home.

I returned back to Germany at the beginning of August, and all I though about during my journey home was being with my family again. It was one of the longest journeys I had ever made. I arrived back at the barracks during the early hours of the morning, and I thought rather than waking Sandra to come and get me, I asked the duty driver in the guardroom if he would be kind enough to give me a lift home. I threw my bags into the back of the Landrover and sat in the passenger seat, excited about being home again. Again, the journey seemed to last an eternity, and we were slowed down by almost every red traffic light on the way. As we entered my street, my heart began to beat harder and faster with excitement, and when the Landrover stopped outside my house I noticed the bedroom light was on. Was Cameron still having problems with sleeping? Sandra did say in one of her letters that he was being quite unsettled. Oh well, daddy's here now.

I dragged my bags out of the Landrover and carried them, one by one to the front door. I waved the driver off then fished out my keys from the side pouch of my rucksack. I quietly opened the door and dragged my bags through to the front room; they could just wait there until later. I took off my boots and quietly crept up the stairs to surprise Sandra. As I walked past Cameron's room, I looked in, and he was fast asleep. I crept up to my bedroom door, and as I grabbed the door handle I could hear noises coming from inside that instantly made my skin crawl.

I swung the door open and stood there staring for what seemed for hours. I could see my Sandra on all fours with a man penetrating her from behind while she gave oral sex to another man in front of her. My heart continued to beat
harder and harder and I could feel my breathing becoming heavier. Subconsciously I clenched both of my fists and slowly walked towards the bed. Both of the men jumped off the bed, still naked, and tried making past me through the door. My fist connected, with a crunch, to the jaw of the man on my left, dropping him to the floor. I then brought my elbow backwards to connect with the other man's chest which winded him and caused him to double up in pain. As he crouched down, I grabbed him by the back of his head and brought my right knee hard into his face, spreading his nose outwards. Before the man on the left fully gained consciousness I grabbed him by his hair and dragged him out of the room to the top of the stairs. Still holding onto his hair, I slammed his face into the wall, knocking him back into a deep sleep. As I turned to go back into the room, the other man ran towards me, but I quickly stepped to one side, and he tripped over his sleeping associate and fell head first down the stairs. He lay at the bottom of the stairs motionless. I then grabbed the sleeping man by his ankles and dragged him down the stairs to join his friend. I left the two men at the bottom of the stairs, went into the living room and put my boots back on. I was totally oblivious to Sandra's and Cameron's screaming upstairs, and I just stepped out the front door and walked.

Although I wasn't sure where I was heading, I found myself walking out of town, into the outskirts and then onto the "route sixty four" which would take me towards Paderborn. There were no footpaths, so I walked aimlessly along the hard shoulder, heading for nowhere in particular. I felt numb and stared into nothingness. My mind was filled with jumbled up thoughts and my head was spinning out of control. I was only wearing combat trousers and a t shirt, and my skin was pimpled due to the early morning chill in the air, but I could not feel the cold. I eventually came across a service station, so I walked into the building and bought myself a bottle of Asbach brandy. I picked some money out of my pocket and threw a twenty Euro note to the assistant, then walked out, not waiting for any change.

    I carried on walking along the road until I saw a sign for a war memorial, so I followed the signs until I
reached the entrance to the cemetery. The gates were closed, so I sat on the grass with my back against the wall and slowly drank the bottle of brandy. This was the first drink I'd had for months, so it wasn't long before I was feeling the effects, and eventually fell asleep with the empty bottle in my hand.

    I eventually woke to the sound of two German police officers walking towards me. I looked at my watch, it was half nine in the morning. The cemetery care taker had apparently come to open up and found me slouched against the wall and called the police. My head was pounding, my mouth was totally dry and my trousers were soaking wet from the morning dew on the grass. As the policemen got nearer, I attempted to stand up, but I was so dizzy I slid back down the wall onto my backside. The policemen picked me up and carried me towards the car. I had no energy to fight them off, and allowed myself to be dragged along and thrown into the back of their car, where I fell asleep again.

    The next thing I remember was waking up in a cell at the German police station and seeing three British military policemen coming to take me back to barracks. I told them I wanted to go back home, but they insisted that I went to barracks due to an incident at my home. After I had left the house, Sandra had rang the military police, and they had apparently spent all night looking for me. I had also apparently caused some serious damage to those two men, and they were both in hospital.

The military policemen escorted me to a cell in the barracks guardroom, and sat me on the hard bed. Two of them stood by the cell door, while the other, who was a sergeant, placed me under arrest.

"Are you 24877151 sergeant Mark Harrison?" the sergeant asked.

"Well if I'm not," I replied, "I'm doing a fucking good impression of him. Yes I am, mate."

The sergeant then continued, "Sergeant Harrison, you are now under arrest for suspected grievous bodily harm, but you're unfit for interview at the moment, so we're going to leave you here under close observation until you sober up. We will come back for you later, and give you a full brief then. For now, you need to get some kip and sort your head out, mate. Okay?"

I looked up and nodded, "Aye, I suppose so. Looking forward to our little chin-wag later actually. Just make sure you get the kettle on. Now if you don't mind, fuck off and let me sleep. Laters."

The sergeant smiled and shook his head as he walked out of the cell, taking his two little monkeys with him. I lay on the hard wooden bed, resting my head on the thin pillow and managed to fall into a deep sleep.

I had been left at the guardroom for over twenty four hours, as the military police were busy piecing together their evidence from my home. Apparently Sandra had complained about not being able to clean up the mess, from where I had left blood stains on the wall upstairs and all the way down the stairs carpet. So the military police did what they had to do so she could clear up the mess and then get on with her dirty, shameful life. The two men had been interviewed from their hospital beds, and claimed that they weren't aware that Sandra was married, despite the fact that she was living in a house that's only married soldiers and their families use. Lying bastards! Sandra had also given a statement to the police, so I was interested to find out what bullshit she fed them when it came to my interview.

It was about ten in the morning when the military policemen returned to the guardroom for me, cuffed me, escorted me to their car and drove to the station. My photograph was taken, a DNA swab from my mouth was taken then they took my fingerprints. Apparently this was routine for all cases, not just mine. I was then ushered into a small soundproof room where I sat in front of two military policemen over a small square wooden table which had a cassette recorder on it.

After pressing the "record" button on the machine and giving the statutory preliminaries, the sergeant opposite me asked, "Right, Sergeant Harrison. You know why you're here, so can we begin by hearing you version of events, please?"

"My version of events?" I replied, "No, I'll tell you what actually happened mate. I got home at daft o'clock the other morning after spending a fucking horrible few months in Iraq. I walked into *my* bedroom to find my wife being fucked by two blokes on *my* bed. So I gave the two twats a good pasting. I left, I got pissed and you found me. Simple as that. Now you tell me how you would react if you caught your wife being spit roasted by two blokes in your own house. You'd want to fucking kill them, wouldn't you?"

The sergeant paused for a fraction of a second, sat back and asked, "So you're saying you intended on killing those two men, Sergeant Harrison?"

"Don't you fucking sit there and twist my words around, you jumped up little prick," my blood was now boiling, "you know exactly what I mean. I know what I saw, and I reacted in the way any other married man would!"

The sergeant leaned forward again, resting his elbows on the table and asked, "You do realise that you're in a lot of trouble here, Sergeant Harrison, for beating up two commissioned officers. You've caused some extensive injuries to both of them."

I leaned forward and rested my elbows on the table so my nose was almost touching the sergeant's, "So this is what it's all about eh?" I asked, "I've kicked the shit out of two Ruperts and now they're hiding behind their fucking rank hoping they'll get away with it? Spineless bastards. One rule for them, another for us."

"It's not like that at all, Sergeant Harrison," he replied, "I appreciate that fact that you'll be feeling angry at the moment. But the issue is that you have beaten up two officers, causing grievous bodily harm. One of them has a fractured jaw, two missing teeth and a hairline fracture on the back of his skull. The officer has a punctured lung due to a broken rib penetrating it, and I don't think he got that from a bit of rough sex with your wife."

Those last few words from the sergeant caused me to see red and I erupted. I stood up, flipping the table over and sending the recording machine and paperwork flying through the air. The sergeant stood up, startled, and I pinned him in the corner pointing in his face.

"Tell you what, sunshine," I spat, "You can take your interview and your little pet monkey over there, and you can shove them up your fucking arse! I'm not taking any more shit from you bunch of jumped up fucking Nazis. You know fine well that I did what anyone else would do, and all you want is a result from me so you can kiss your commanding officer's arse and show him how much of a good little policeman you've been. So if it's a result you need, I suggest you get me a fucking solicitor because you're not getting another fucking word out of me."

I sat back down in my chair, folded my arms across my chest and asked, "You got a fag I can have? I'm fucking gasping."

The sergeant crept out of his corner, picked up the recording machine and whimpered, "Interview terminated."

I was escorted back to a cell at the guard room, and the

door was locked behind me. Half an hour or so later, the guard commander opened the door hatch and said, "Hey Sarge, the guard are off to the cook house for their dinner, and was wondering if you want one of them to bring you something back to eat."

I looked up at the young corporal as he peered through the hatch, and I could see he was scared. He had obviously heard about what happened. "Aye, please mate," I replied, "I wouldn't say no to a brew either if I'm not pushing my luck."

The corporal gave me a thumbs up through the hatch, and as he walked off I heard him shout into the guard's rest room, "Someone make a brew for the sergeant out the back, and make it quick, it looks like he needs it!"

Another hour had passed when the cell door swung open, and the corporal walked in carrying a plastic tray. He placed the tray on the floor by the side of my bed, and I could see a plate full of bacon, eggs, sausage and beans, and a hot steaming mug of coffee. I looked up at him and he showed me a nervous smile.

"You heard what happened then, eh?" I asked him.

"Yes I did sarge," he replied after a short pause, "and forgive me for saying this, but from what I've heard, those two fuckers deserved more than what they got. If you ask me, they're fucking lucky they're still breathing."

I smiled back at him and said, "Well I can assure you that I'm no nutter mate, so there's no need to be nervous around me. I just blew my top when I saw what was going on. I don't normally make a habit out of kicking the shit out of someone for the hell of it."

"Nah, it's fair enough sarge," he said, "I would've done the same if it was me in your shoes. It's just a fucking shame you're probably not going to get away with it."

"Oh, I know I'm in the shit mate," I replied, "looks like I'm going to get screwed over big time. But I'll tell you something, I ain't going down without a fucking fight."

The corporal gave me a wink and said, "Well I wish you the best of British, and I really mean that. Anyway, I'll leave you to it, enjoy your dinner and just give me a shout if here's anything you need."

He walked out the cell and closed the door behind him. Seconds later I could hear him shouting at one of the younger soldiers to make him a coffee. I looked down at the tray and the food actually looked quite appetising. There must be a decent chef on shift today in the cook house. I picked up the tray and placed it on my knee. I began to eat and within seconds the meal was demolished. The coffee was obviously a cheap brand, but I didn't mind because it was warm, wet and sweet.

After I finished my coffee I felt full and content, so I lay back on the bed, put my hands over my head, and I was just about to doze off when the cell door swung open again. It was my commanding officer, Colonel Smythe.

"What the bloody hell have you been playing at, Sergeant Harrison?" He boomed as he sat on the bed next to me.

"Well, erm, I'm sure you've been told what happened, sir." I replied.

The Colonel leaned towards me and went on, "Yes, but let's hear your side of the story, sunshine."

I stood up and cleared my throat, "Sir, to cut a long story short, I caught two of your boys humping my missus, so I gave them a kicking."

The Colonel shook his head, "You're better than that though, sergeant. You've worked damn hard to get where you are, and you've just thrown it all away. There's not a lot I can do to help you here, but if it makes you feel any better, I will be charging my two officers for what they did. I don't want to make you feel any worse, but I've got a feeling you're going to have the book thrown at you, and they'll make an example of you."

I smirked and shrugged my shoulders then said, "And I suppose you're going to make an example of your boys for screwing my wife in my house, while they all thought I was away? Or will they be given a slap on the wrist and post them out somewhere out of the way?"

The Colonel frowned, and then stood up, putting his hand on my shoulder. Don't you worry about those two, I will deal with that. I've had a word with the police and I've managed to pull a few strings. If you agree to stay away from your home and your wife for now, the police will allow you to stay on the barracks. And that's also on the condition that you don't do anything bloody stupid. Stay on camp, go to work as usual. I think you need to keep yourself occupied, and don't go daft. If need be, I will get a couple of the guard to escort you to your house so you can collect your things and help you move into the sergeants' mess. Okay?"

I nodded and replied, "Aye, thanks sir. And don't worry I won't go mental on anyone."

"Right then," he said, "get a few hours sleep, you look like hell. And I will arrange for you to go to sort your things out in the morning after breakfast."

I bolted up off the bed and stood to attention, "Thanks again, sir."

The Colonel walked to the cell door, stopped and turned to face me and said, "Don't thank me sergeant, because this is just the beginning of a long hard slog. I will do what I can to help, but as far as GBH is concerned, my hands are tied. Sort yourself out with a solicitor as soon as you can."

He turned and walked out the cell, calling for the guard commander to lock up. The corporal popped his head around the door, gave me a thumbs up then closed me in. I despised the sound of that door slamming shut.

I didn't sleep much that night as I lay thinking of what had happened. My head was spinning with trying to understand why Sandra would do such a thing. The images of what I witnessed were stuck solid in my mind and I couldn't shake them away. I had known Sandra since our school days, and I never, for one moment, thought she was capable of doing something so vile and thoughtless. My son was sleeping in the bedroom next door for God's sake!

Emerging from my mixed up thoughts, I could feel hatred rearing its ugly head, and all I could feel was anger for what she did. Was she thinking of me while she was doing it? Or was she just laughing about it, thinking it was all a big joke. Was she sober?

Then I started blaming myself. Should I have contacted her from the airport, letting her know I'm home? I would've been none the wiser if I had given her time. Did she do it because I was away so much on operations and exercise and she was feeling lonely? Did I over react when I walked into the bedroom?

The questions spun around in my head, over and over, and I could not answer any of them. Then my thoughts focused onto my little boy. Would I see him again? Will he grow up hating me? Will he be told the truth about me?

As I could see the sun rising through my cell window, I could feel myself slowly drifting off to sleep, so I turned onto my side facing the wall and slept for an hour or so before the guard commander woke me for breakfast. I was too tired to face any food, so I asked for just a coffee and a cigarette. I walked out of the cell, along the short corridor and turned right into the old exercise yard. As I lit a cigarette, the guard commander came out with my coffee. He passed the cup over to me then stood against the wall next to me. "I hear they're letting you back to work today, sarge."

"Aye, looks that way mate. But I can't see the OC letting me into the armoury to handle weapons, do you?"

"Ha ha," he laughed, "you got a point there like. Don't want you going on a rampage or anything."

The corporal froze and appeared to have stopped breathing for a few brief moments after he realised what he had just said. His face drained of its entire colour.

I stepped in front of him, put my hand on his shoulder and said, "Don't flap mate, I might be in the shit, but I've still got my sense of humour."

The corporal took a few more drags from his cigarette, stubbed what was left of it into the wall, apologised for what he said and walked back into the guard room.

It was about ten o'clock when my cell door swung open, and the provost sergeant came in, waving his pace stick about in my face and shouted, "Come on then sergeant, time to go and sort your fucking life out. Two of my guard are waiting outside with the duty driver to take you home for your things!"

I continued to lie on the bed with my hands behind my head, staring at the provost sergeant, for a few seconds before I slowly got myself up from the bed. I took a few steps towards him, making him back up against the wall, and I said, "First of all, I'm not fucking deaf, so quit the shouting. Secondly, I'm not one of your fucking little minions who you talk to like they're a piece of shit on your shoe. I'm still a fucking sergeant. And while I'm here, if you point that fucking stick at me one more time, I'll shove it so far down your throat it'll pop out your arse."

"You can't speak to me like that!" he continued to bellow, "I'm the fucking provost sergeant, which makes me senior to you!"

"Yes," I replied, "and do you know why you're the provost sergeant? Because you're fucking useless at any other job you get given, so they've stuck you in the guard room out the way. Now I suggest you step aside out my way, and let me get on with my things, otherwise that fucking stick will be going where the sun doesn't shine. Now fuck off, and go polish up some artillery shells or summit!"

I stepped out of the cell and saw the two young soldiers who were "specially" chosen to help me get my things. They had just witnessed me pulling shreds from the provost sergeant, and their faces were turning purple with struggling not to laugh.

"Right lads," I said to them, "let's get out of this shit hole, and take me home."

The house felt empty. All the furniture was still there, but it just felt like a lifeless shell. Sandra must be at work and Cameron must be at nursery. The two young lads remained by the open front door as I wandered around my house. Although everything was still where I had left it, it felt so different. I felt like a stranger in someone else's home. I walked to the foot of the stairs and as I looked up I could see the faded line all the way up the carpet where Sandra must have scrubbed away the blood stains. The wall at the top of the stairs also had a faded patch where it had been cleaned. For almost a fraction of a second, I felt sorry for leaving Sandra to clean up my mess. But that rapidly left my head, and I returned the continuing numbness. The last few drops of emotion had been drained from me, and I felt nothing.

I packed a few things into black bin liners and asked the two lads to throw them into the back of the Landrover while I sat in my son's room for a while. The décor in his room was just how I left it. The walls were painted a sunshine yellow and white cotton candy clouds mobiles hung from the ceiling above his cot. I picked up his little yellow pillow and I could smell him on it. But why was I not crying? I hadn't seen my son for months, and although I'm back home, I still can't see him. I walked out of his room and into my bedroom, I stood at the door and the images of what I saw rushed into my head again. This was not helping me; I needed to get away from here. As I turned and headed down the stairs, I saw a familiar figure come through the front door, pushing the young soldiers aside. It was Sandra, and she didn't look too pleased to see me.

"What the fuck are you doing here, you psycho?" she screamed.

I continued to walk down the stairs and looked at her in disbelief at what she had just said. The two young soldiers stepped forwards to intervene, and I signalled them to go and wait outside. I squared up close to Sandra, still emotionless, but staring into her eyes and gave her a reply, "Me? Psycho? Remind me of what I saw in the bedroom the other morning. Was I seeing things? Or were you being shagged rotten by two Ruperts?"

She continued to scream at me, "You were never here for me Mark, and I had needs. I needed some fun, and you couldn't give me it!"

I shook my head in disbelief, and as I barged past her to walk out the door, I turned to get the final word in, "You really are on in a fucking million, Sandra. And I can really promise you one thing. Once this is all over, I'm coming to get my boy, because you don't deserve to be a mother. You're a dirty fucking whore. Now stay away from me, and rot in hell."

That was the last time I saw Sandra for quite some time.

For the next two months or so I was allowed into work, but I was not permitted to work with weapons unsupervised. That was understandable, I suppose. I wasn't allowed to carry out any guard duties, due to the fact that I would have access to quite a large number of SA80s and ammunition. So if I wasn't working, I was in the gymnasium working out. I was also sensible enough to keep myself away from the bar in the sergeants' mess, because I knew that if I had a drink, all hell would break loose.

On the third of November I appeared before the judge advocate for my preliminary hearing. I sat on the right with my barrister, who was as useful as a handbrake on a canoe, and my advising officer who wished he was somewhere else.

The prosecution stood up and gave their evidence, half of which was total fabricated bullshit. Apparently, the two men I beat up had tried to reason with me as they did not know she was married. At no point did they try to escape. Bollocks! Also. One of the officers was so badly traumatised from the whole incident, that he resigned from the army, and the other officer had been posted abroad. So much for the Colonel sorting them out. Spineless bastards! The prosecution then went on to spew out more crap abut me being a bad husband, and how I used to physically abuse my wife. I'd never laid a finger on Sandra I in my life! This whole case was a total farce, and they were milking it to make sure I got screwed over good and proper.

After my barrister stood to give my defence, I thought it would have been better if I got my son to represent me. His pitiful speech lasted a whole three minutes and consisted of how much stress I had been through during my recent tour of Iraq, and that the court should take into account the shock I must have experienced when I walked in on Sandra and the two officers.

The judge then asked me to stand, and asked for my plea against the charges of grievous bodily harm and assault against two commissioned officers. And of course, I pleaded guilty because I knew I didn't have a cat in hell's chance of walking away from this in one piece. After a brief pause, the judge informed us that sentencing would take place the next day at eleven o'clock. I suppose I was getting one more night of freedom. I left the court martial centre at half two that afternoon and by seven o'clock that evening I was slumped on my bed in a drunken stupor.

My alarm went off at half six the next morning, and I dragged my sorry carcass out of bed and had a nice long soak in the shower in an attempt to revive myself. After getting dressed into my dress uniform and best boots, I walked down to the mess canteen and forced some breakfast down my throat, as I had a slight inkling that this would be my last decent meal for quite some time. I still had a few hours to waste, so I went back to my room and packed the last of my belongings into a box. All of my military equipment and clothing was packed away on one side of the room in boxes, and what little civilian clothing I had was packed into three bags at the foot of my bed. I sat on the edge of my bed, and reached under it for the bottle of brandy I had been saving for moments like this. I twisted the cap off and took several large gulps of the fiery liquid and felt the warm burning sensation as it slowly poured down my throat into my stomach. After a few more mouthfuls I could feel the numbness return, and I began to relax. Before I felt myself drifting off, I pulled myself together and stood up, checked myself over in the mirror, and then made my way over to the guard room.

When the duty driver dropped the tailgate of the Landrover for me to climb in, I laughed and said to him, "Look mate, if you think I'm climbing into the back of there dressed like this you've got another thing coming."

I walked to the passenger door and looked in, and to my amusement, I saw the provost sergeant sitting there. I opened the door, and leaned forward to whisper, so as not to embarrass him in front of the young driver, "And you can think again if you think you're sitting there. Fuck off into the back."

I climbed onto the passenger seat, and as soon as the provost sergeant mad himself comfortable in the back, we set off for the court martial centre.

The court room was already busy when I arrived, and I noticed that some of my work colleagues had come along and were sitting at the back. As I entered the room and marched down the walkway towards my table, some of them called my name and wished me luck. I was going to fucking need more than luck. I sat at my table, between the two escorts who had been chosen to prevent me from doing a runner. My barrister and advising officer were sat behind me. As I looked at my watch to check how much more freedom I had left, the door in front of us swung open and in walked the judge advocate. We were ordered to stand, but I struggled to stay up as my legs had given way beneath me. I wasn't sure if this was due to the alcohol I drank earlier, or if it was because I was shitting my pants in fear.

The judge ushered everyone to sit as he, in turn, sat at his desk facing us. He spent what seemed like an hour or so shuffling through papers on his desk, before removing his glasses and looking up at me.

"Sergeant Harrison, please stand up." the judge requested firmly.

I slowly took to my feet and left my hands on the desk so I could lean for support. I looked up at the judge and acknowledged him, "Yes sir?"

The judge began his long, drawn out speech, "Sergeant Harrison, I sincerely hope that you realise the seriousness of this case that has been put before me. The sentence you can receive for this is five years imprisonment. I have studied the facts hard and have come to several conclusions. I do appreciate the fact that you have experienced some stressful situations during your operational tour of Iraq, and I commend you for your hard work out there. I have read your past reports and character references, and you have developed into an excellent soldier and tradesman over the years. I am also aware of the shock you must have experienced when coming back home to your wife. But what I certainly do not condone is the violent crime you have committed against these two men. You have been in situations previously where you have had to control your emotions and manage your anger, but in this particular incident, you lost control. You allowed your emotions to take over and run wild. I have also been made aware that, since your arrest, you have shown similar signs of aggression towards figures of authority, including the military police and your provost sergeant. As I have already stated, this offence can carry a sentence of five years imprisonment......"

The judge paused and looked down at his paperwork. I could feel my heart pounding through my chest, harder and faster, and when I looked down I could actually see it beating through my jacket. I could feel the colour drain away from my face, and my legs were turning to jelly, putting more and more strain on my arms that were already struggling to support my bodyweight. "For fuck sake," I thought to myself, "will you just hurry up before I flake out."

He eventually looked back up at me, took a deep breathe and continued, "….. In my professional opinion, giving you a custodial sentence would only worsen your condition and send you further down the spiral you are already descending on, and this leaves me only one choice. I believe that your actions were impulsive and that you were not fully in control of your emotions. But, as a professional, you are aware that this is an inappropriate manner in which to react, and that you should have followed the proper channels of discipline. Unfortunately, and despite you excellent previous character, you have shown no remorse towards your actions and have caused some serious damage. Taking all of this into account, I have not choice but to reduce you to the ranks and discharge you from service with immediate effect. I also suggest that you attend some sort of counselling to tackle you aggression issues, and simply hope that you see this as an opportunity to sort yourself out and get your life back on track. You may think otherwise at the moment, Sergeant Harrison, but I have been rather lenient towards you, and you have had a lucky escape."

The judge then stood up to leave, and everyone in the room rose to their feet. My legs finally gave up the struggle, and my arms were too weak to hold my weight and I collapsed onto the chair behind me. As I watched the judge walk out of the room, my head began to spin again, and I could feel myself slowly lose consciousness.

I eventually came round as the two escorts were struggling to pick me up out of the chair. Some of my work colleagues ran over to help and wished me luck again. I felt lost.

The escorts assisted me back into the Landrover and onto the passenger seat. The provost sergeant was nowhere in sight, spineless bastard! Although the journey back to the barracks only lasted a few minutes, I slept all of the way.

I spent the next few days returning my military equipment and clothing back to the stores, and my last few nights were spent in the bar with my work colleagues. Sandra and Cameron had already moved back to England, and I was about to follow suit, but not to be with them. I had arranged with my mother for me to live with her until I was sorted with a job and somewhere of my own to live.

On the morning of my final day, I was to hand in my identity card at the admin office. I walked into regimental headquarters and along the long corridor to the last office on the right. After waiting a few minutes, one of the office clerks called me over and gave me some paperwork to sign, then I handed him my identity card. Not a word was passed between us, apart from when he explained about me still being bound by the Official Secrets Act. As I walked back down the corridor, a familiar voice boomed out of one of the other offices. It was Colonel Smythe calling for me, but I continued to walk.

"Sergeant Harrison?" the colonel shouted as he poked his head out of his office door. "Did you not hear me?"

I stopped and slowly turned to face him, and as I walked towards him I replied, "Sorry, I think you've got me mixed up with someone else. I'm *Mr* Mark Harrison, not *Sergeant* Harrison."

Totally ignoring my bitterness, the colonel turned and walked into his office, saying, "Come on in Mark, I want to see you before you go."

I stood at the doorway of the colonel's office and watched him walk behind his enormous oak desk and sit in his leather chair.

"No thanks," I said, "I'll stay here if it's all the same."

"Fair enough," the colonel continued, "I only wanted to see that you're okay".

"Okay?" my voice was now raised, "Check to see if I'm

okay? I've just been fucked over by the army. I've just lost everything, and you're asking if I'm okay? I'll guarantee that within a couple of years, those two cunts will have been promoted to captain or something. Everything will have been forgotten about, because the big nasty sergeant has gone!"

The colonel stood up and began to talk, "Now listen here....."

"No, you fucking listen to me!" I barked, "It's always been the same. One set of rules for you fucking officers, and a different set of rules for us. Now at the moment, I feel like I've got nothing to lose, so I suggest you sit down before I fucking put you down!"

My screaming had brought attention in the corridor, and as I turned to look, I noticed that the regimental sergeant major had come storming out of his office towards me.

"And before you get on your fucking high horse," I bellowed at the sergeant major before he had the chance to speak. "You even open your mouth and I'll fucking hit you with him."

The colonel and sergeant major had both froze and were dumb struck as they looked at each other, hoping for some sort of support from each other. Before I exploded, I turned and continued walking out of the corridor, nudging my shoulder against the sergeant major as I passed. As I opened the main entrance door, I turned to see both of them stood in the corridor, staring at me in disbelief. The door slammed behind me.

I walked down to the guardroom where I had left my bags, and without saying a word to anyone, I picked them up and stormed back out. Just as I walked out of the main gates of the barracks, I dropped my bags, turned round to face the regiment and stuck a middle finger in the air.

The taxi taking me to the airport seemed to take forever, but as soon as it arrived, I threw my bags into the boot and climbed into the back. Not once did I look back as the taxi pulled away. I made the long hard journey back to "Civvy Street".

Chapter 3

The journey from Germany back to England seemed to take forever, and of course my flight from Hannover was delayed by three hours, so that didn't really help matters. Once I had collected my baggage from the conveyor belt, I pushed my trolley through the exit, and out into the cold. Typical British weather; pissing down. A taxi screeched to a halt in front of me and I threw my bags into the boot, and then climbed into the back of the car.

"Sunderland, please mate." I mumbled to the driver.

He looked in his rear view mirror, and noticed that I didn't look very happy, so he just gave me a smile and pulled away.

After about ten minutes or so, the driver broke the silence. It was obviously killing him. "You on leave, son? Just that I noticed a couple of army bags going in the boot there."

"Nah mate," I said as I stared out the window, "I've just left for good."

"Well, if you ask me, son," he continued, "think you've had a lucky escape, what with all that shite going on over in Iraq. They' shouldn't even be there, I'm telling you."

I looked over into his mirror and stared into his eyes. "I'd rather not talk about it, if it's all the same."

The driver raised his eyebrows and shrugged his shoulders, and carried on driving along the motorway.

The rest of the journey was spent in total silence, and I gave out a huge sigh of relief when we pulled up outside my mother's house. I handed him the fare, got out the car and pulled my bags out the boot. The second the boot was slammed shut, the taxi was gone, and as I picked up my bags, the front door of my mother's house opened. There she stood waiting, with tears rolling down her face.

I walked up to the house, and as soon as I reached the door I had to drop my bags when my mother wrapped her arms around me tightly and whispered, "It's good to have you home at last, son."

    I just smiled, picked up my bags and dragged them into the hallway. My mother followed me into the living room and stood watching as I sunk into the big black leather sofa. I dropped my head back and closed my eyes. As I relaxed, I could feel the tears rolling down my cheeks. My mother sat next to me, and when I looked, I could see that she was in tears also.

    "I'll get there, mam," I reassured her, "I'll be okay once I get over the shock of what's happened."

    Mum smiled and replied, "Well, some of the lads are coming round to see you after tea. They want to celebrate having you back home."

    "Any excuse for a piss up," I said, almost smiling.

    Mum moved closer to and put her arm around me and pulled me in close, "Look son, there's no rush for you to do anything yet. Just take your time, and remember that this is your home. So stay as long as you want. In fact, I've gone long enough with you being away, so I want to make the most of having you back. Give it a few days, then get yourself down to the job centre to sign on, but don't worry about money for now, that's not an issue. And don't rush into finding a job either, just get yourself settled in first, okay?"

    She held onto me tightly and gave me a reassuring pat on the shoulder, before getting up to go into the kitchen. I might be a thirty six year old, hairy arsed ex squaddie, but I still missed my mother's cuddles.

    It wasn't long before I could smell the inviting aroma of grilled bacon oozing out f the kitchen, so I walked to the door and leaned against the wall while I watched mum buzz around her little kitchen, making me a bacon sandwich.

    "There's only one thing I want you to do, Mark," mum said as she pottered around, "my grandson is back in Sunderland, and I don't want to miss out on any more time with him than I already have to. You know what I mean?"

"Oh, I know mam," I replied, "he's just had his third birthday, and I don't want him to grow up thinking I don't care. Don't worry mam, I'll find out where he is."

My mother paused and looked at me with raised eyebrows, "Yes, do find out where he lives, but don't anything stupid. A little dickybird told me that Sandra and Cameron are somewhere in Castletown, but I couldn't tell you exactly whereabouts. Just do what you can without causing any trouble."

I was about to say "okay" to my mother when the telephone in the hallway began to ring. I picked up the receiver and answered. It was my mate, Jez, checking to see if I was home. He told me that he and some of the lads were coming to take me out for a few drinks at about seven o'clock. I hung up and went through the living room into the dining room where my bacon sandwich and mug of coffee were waiting for me on the table.

After I had eaten, I carried my bags upstairs to my old room, and when I kicked the door open, I saw all the military photos that I had sent to my mother over the years plastered all over the walls. It was like a military museum. I threw my bags onto the bed and opened them, emptying the contents into a big pile. In amongst the pile I found Cameron's little pillow that I had taken from his room back in Germany, so I placed it on my pillow. I put an old framed photograph of me holding Cameron the day I flew out to Iraq onto my bedside table. I sorted out my clothes and hung them in the old pine wardrobe, and then threw the empty bags under the bed. I then lay on the bed, reached over for the TV remote control and watched an old black and white movie, which eventually sent me off into a nice deep sleep.

Jez and the lads had come for me just as I was getting out of the shower. They were half an hour early. I could hear them in the living room talking to my mother as I rushed to get ready. My mother thought the world of my friends, but they could be a bit of a handful at times, and sometimes be even quite cheeky towards her. In a playful way though. Jez had, on quite a number of occasions, felt the palm of my mother's hand on the back of his head for letting his mouth go.

Jez and I go right back a far as primary school. Our initial meeting was quite odd, as we were fighting over a football in the school yard. Still to this day, Jez reckons he got the better of me, but it was his nose that was bleeding, not mine. We were actually forced by our teachers to become friends and since then we became inseparable. Some people called us "Ronnie and Reggie", as we sometimes caused havoc whenever we got together. When we moved up to secondary school together, two became four when Nick and Lurch joined us. Lurch's real name was Paul, but he resembles the butler from the old "Addams Family" TV program, and the names has stuck ever since. Together we were like a team, rather than a group of mates, and we did everything together.

When I married Sandra, I couldn't decide who to ask to be my best man, so all three of them took on the role. This was a bad move, on my behalf, because they had put their heads together to give one hell of a best man's speech. They tore me to shreds.

Once I was dressed I ran downstairs and walked into the living room where the lads were. As soon as I opened the living room door, the three of them were on their feet and surrounded me. I think they were pleased to see me, in a manly way though. I could see my mother standing back, watching us and smiling. She had her boys back, just like the old days.

Mum was kind enough to offer us a lift into town, so I got into the back with Nick and Jez, while Lurch sat in the front next to my mother. Lurch always has to sit in the front because of his legs being so damn long. Lurch turned up the radio and we began to sing along to Duran Duran's "Rio".

A few seconds into the song, Lurch turned around to face us, "That reminds me," he grunted, "there's an eighties night on over at Liberties tonight. Reckon we should go there cos there's bound to be loads of totty knocking about."

"Lurch man," Nick replied with a smile, "who the fuck's going to want to go anywhere near you, unless she's about eight foot tall, with a hump on her back and in a coffin during the day."

We all burst into laughter, apart from Lurch of course, "Well you can all go fuck yourselves, " he cursed as he turned round to face the front.

"Tell you what lads," mum added, "if I hear anyone else using language like that again in front of me again, you'll get the back of my hand."

"Sorry mam." we all replied in unison.

We walked into the club together, but had to wait a few minutes while Lurch received the obligatory body search from the doorman. It always happened to him. Then after paying our admission we handed our jackets over to the cloakroom attendant. As we entered the main part of the club, it felt like we had stepped back in time by about twenty years. Some of the women were wearing fluorescent leg warmers, rah rah skirts and back combed hair, and even some of the men were dressed for the occasion in chinos and "Frankie says relax" t-shirts. During my discharge medical from the army, I was warned of the possibility of flashbacks, but I had no idea it would be as freaky as this. We found a small round table that looked over the dance floor, and we spent the next few minutes arguing over who was going to get the first round of drinks in. Nick, Jez and Lurch insisted that I wasn't to pay for anything as it was my "welcome home" piss up, but they could not decide amongst themselves who was buying first. Before I began dehydrating in anticipation, I stood up and walked to the bar and ordered four bottles of beer. I walked back to the table and slammed the beers down, saying, "There you go girls, have a drink while you're bickering over the next round.

"We were going to get them in man, Mark." Nic said after gulping down half of his beer.

"Aye," I replied, "but if I had waited until you had finished bitching, I would've died of thirst."

Once we got into the routine of who was buying what and when, the booze began to flow. It felt good being with my old friends again, and it felt like I had never been away. The only difference was, it felt like the lads were walking around on egg shells, trying their best not to upset me by slipping up and mentioning the army.

Lurch looked across the dance floor then back at us, "Hey lads," he said excitedly, "reckon we should all get up for a bit of a boogie. There's loads of fanny on the dance floor. Who's up for it?"

"Nah thank mate," I replied, "not really in the mood for making a twat of myself quite yet. I just wanna get shit faced tonight."

"Well I'm not getting up with you, daft arse," Nick added, "I'd look fucking stupid dancing next to you, you lanky streak of piss."

"Cheeky twat," Lurch went on, "you don't need to stand next to me to look fucking stupid, you fucking ginger bastard."

Jez almost fell backwards off his chair with laughter, and almost choked on his beer. "Ha ha, fucking classic, Lurch. You kill me sometimes mate. You might look like a dumb arse, but you're sharp as fuck. Fucking love you mate."

"Well I have to be sharp with that twat, don't I?" Lurch moaned as he stood up, "Anyway, bollocks to you lot, I'm off onto the dance floor. Give me a shout when it's my round."

We watched Lurch as he trundled off to the middle of the dance floor and laughed as he showed us his moves.

"Look at that," Nick laughed, "he's the only bloke I know who dances without moving his arms. They're just hanging there. Big dopey twat."

"Ah, just leave him man," said Jez, "as long as he's enjoying himself. You know what he's like after a few drinks, loves a bit of a dance. And I tell you what, if you keep winding him up the way you are, he's going to take you're fucking head off one of these days. His hands are like fucking shovels. Anyway, my round. You all having the same?"

Before we even had the chance to answer, Jez was up and off to the bar. A few minutes later he came back, placed the beers on the table, and when he sat down he leaned towards me and whispered, "Think we might have to keep our eye on those knob heads over there at the bar, mate. I heard them taking the piss out of Lurch."

I looked across to the bar and saw three men stood there, and it looked like they were pointing at laughing at Lurch.

"Ah, this is the last fucking thing I could do with," I moaned, "but we'll keep an eye on them, and they start anything, we'll finish it."

After another two songs had been played, Lurch came back to the table, sat down and took a swig from his beer. "God, it bloody warm on that dance floor." He said whilst mopping his brow, "I'm sweating like Hitler when he got his gas bill."

He took another mouthful of his beer and stood up again, "Well, I'm off to drain the snake. I'll get the beers in on the way back, okay?"

Lurch trundled off again, but this time around the edge of the dance floor to the toilets at the back of the room. I looked across to the bar and saw the three men gulp down their beers and head towards the toilets also.

"Well lads," I said, downing my beer, "I think things are about to get fucking interesting. Follow me to the bogs and wait outside the door. If anyone tries coming in, stop them."

The three of us walked around the dance floor, and when we got to the toilet entrance I reminded them to stop anyone from getting in after me. I slowly walked in, and quietly closed the door behind me, making sure it didn't slam behind me. I saw Lurch standing at a urinal and two of the men were stood either side of him. The other man was sat on a bin on the left and I could hear him making comments to his friends about the size of Lurch. I headed towards the sinks on the left, and as I was washing my hands I kept on eye on Lurch through the mirrors.

The man who was sat on the bin stood up and walked towards Lurch. "Hey, lanky twat," he slurred, "you look like a right fucking retard. What's the weather like up there?"

Lurch zipped himself up and turned with his back to the urinal to face him. The men either side of him turned inwards. Lurch then looked down at the man in front of him and then to the others either side of him. He then looked back at the man in front of him and replied, "And I take it you're a jumped up little prick with small man's syndrome."

The two men either side of Lurch grabbed his arms to pin him against the wall, and before the other could react I ran at him from behind. I grabbed him by his collar and threw him back and to the left, hurling through a toilet cubicle door. The man who was holding onto Lurch's right arm then felt my fist crunch into his nose, making him release his grip. Once he was free, Lurch slammed the palm of his right hand into the face of the man that was still holding onto him. He dropped to the floor and was out cold. "Small bloke syndrome" man came staggering out of the cubicle, so Lurch drew back his right arm and punched him square in the chest, sending him flying back into the cubicle.

As me and Lurch turned to run out of the toilets, the entrance door swung open and Jez popped his head through, "Shift your arses," he began to shout, "looks like the bouncers are coming over."

We sprinted out of the toilets, Jez and Nick following. We ran straight across the dance floor, knocking some people over in the process, and headed for the club's exit.

"What about our jackets, Mark?" asked Lurch as we were running towards the door.

"Fuck the jackets. I'll buy you a new one if you want," I

replied, "let's just get the fuck out of here."

We all managed to escape from the club unscathed, but we continued to run until we reached the taxi rank. By the time we got there, Nick, Jez and Lurch were totally breathless. Thankfully, there was no queue for a taxi so I opened the back door of one of the cabs, "Come on lads," I ordered, "jump in the back of this one, and I'll get in the front."

I climbed onto the front seat f the cab, and when I heard the back door slam shut, I looked at the driver and said, "The Blue Bell please, mate."

By the time the taxi had reached the Blue Bell pub, everyone had managed to catch their breathe and calm down. We walked into the quiet bar room, found a small table in the corner and sat down.

I then turned to Lurch and said, "Right mate, I do believe it's your round. Make mine a fucking double!"

Chapter 4

I was rudely awoken by the sound of letters being pushed through the letterbox and falling onto the doorstep in the hallway. I rolled over and looked at the alarm clock. It was twenty past eleven. Well, I must've needed the sleep. I crawled out of bed and dragged myself downstairs wearing only my boxer shorts. I picked up the mail and noticed two letters were addressed to me. I walked into the kitchen and made myself a coffee. Out of the pile of letters I picked out the two addressed to me, picked up my mug of coffee and walked through into the living room.

The high pitched shriek almost made me drop my coffee. "Sorry mam, sorry aunty Linda." I said sheepishly, "I'll go and make myself decent shall I?"

"Aye son," mum said with a smile, "that would be good."

I went back to my room and threw a pair of tracksuit bottoms and a t-shirt on then went back downstairs. Although they were both laughing, Aunty Linda's face was still a dark shade of red, so I apologised again.

I sat at the dining table, took a sip from my coffee and began opening my mail. The first letter was from the job centre confirming my appointment for next week so I can sign on. The other letter was from Sandra, but there was no address. I took another sip from my coffee before reading it.

Dear Mark. Nice to see you got yourself back home and I'm glad you didn't go down for what happened back in Germany. But I must say that you were bang out of order for the way you went on. You could have killed those lads. It just wasn't like you at all.

Because of what happened, and because of the way you reacted, I will be filing for divorce on the grounds of unreasonable behaviour. I'm also going to mention to my solicitor about the way you have been because I think it could affect my son. At the moment, I don't think it's a good idea for you to see him, because I don't know who you are any more. You're a violent man, Mark.

Also, I would like you to sort out some sort of maintenance to pay towards the upkeep of Cameron, seems as I'm not working yet. We can come to some sort of agreement, or I can leave it to the Child Support Agency to sort out

If you need to contact me, just go via my mam and dad, they will forward any messages from you to me. You also might want to get yourself a solicitor so that we can sort this out properly. Sandra."

I read the letter over two or three times before I actually digested what she had written. I couldn't believe it; she was stopping me from seeing my son because f the way I reacted when I caught her shagging about! She's the one in the wrong, not me.

My mother knew there was something wrong by the look of disbelief on my face. She stood up from the sofa and walked towards me. "I won't ask what's in the letter, son." she said, "but if you need any help, just let me know, okay?"

Before walking back over to her seat, mum put her hand on my shoulder and kissed my head. As she sat next to Aunt Linda, I looked up at them both and said, "Well I'll leave the letter there on the table, and I don't mind you reading it. In fact, I'd like you to read it, and then at least you'll know what I have to put up with. She's nothing but a snake with tits."

I finished off what was left of my coffee and went back upstairs to get dressed. My head began spinning and the old feeling of numbness was returning. The deep rooted images of Sandra and those two men together re emerged in my head, but this time, in the images, they were laughing at me. In my mind, I looked down at the man lying at the bottom of the stairs, and he rose to his feet, looked up at me, and began laughing hysterically. I then turned at the top of the stairs to face Cameron's room, and when I opened the door I could see him standing up in his cot, pointing and laughing at me.

I lay on my bed and closed my eyes in the hope that the images would disappear, and eventually they did fade. But the voices were still there, laughing and mocking. I could feel my head spin faster and faster, and it wasn't long before nausea was setting in. The voices were gradually becoming louder and I suddenly sat bolt upright and screamed at the top of my voice, "Fuck off! Just leave me alone!"

My screams had obviously startled my mother and Aunt Linda, and within seconds they both burst through my bedroom door. They saw me lay on my bed curled up in the foetal position, sobbing uncontrollably into Cameron's pillow. They both knelt on the floor by the side of my bed facing me, and my mother started stroking my hair.

"Look son," she said, "I know you're a grown man now, and you've probably seen and done things that would give any other man nightmares for the rest of their life. But you're still my boy. If that bitch thinks she can mess with my family, she's got me to deal with first. I've read your letter, and I'm not letting her or any snotty nosed solicitor fuck you up any more than you already are."

I looked up at her, and although the tears continued to roll, my crying gradually turned into laughter.

"What you laughing at, you daft bugger?" aunt Linda asked.

I replied, "My mam's just used the F-word."

My mother had left me to sleep, and after two or three hours, I woke up feeling a little bit better. Those vile images and voices had gone from my head, and the numbness had also disappeared. In fact, I was feeling rather bloody good, for once. I stuck my head out of the bedroom door and shouted to see if anyone was about. Quiet. I walked downstairs in just my boxer shorts, and made myself another coffee in the kitchen. On the way into the living room, I picked up the cordless telephone from the hallway and sat on the big leather sofa. My mother didn't like anyone sat on her sofa when holding a drink, but I wasn't causing any harm, so what the hell.

I took a few sips from my coffee, and then carefully placed the cup on he floor by my feet. I punched a few buttons on the phone and waited.

Jez gave his usual welcome message, "Eh up mate, what can I do you for?"

"I'm after a little favour mate, if you're not too busy." I replied.

I heard Jez give out a small sigh before he answered, "Depends what you're after mate. I've just got in from shift and I'm covered in shite still."

Oh I don't mean right now," I said, "just within the next five minutes or so."

Jez grunted, "Funny fucker. Tell you what; give me an hour or so. I'll grab a quick shower then I'll pop round. Is that okay, sir?"

"Hey, you're a scholar and a gentleman, Jez. Ta mate." I grovelled.

"Aye I know," Jez continued, "that's my problem sometimes. Right I'll be round in a bit, so get the kettle on the boil, shit brick."

Jez hung up, so I went into the hallway and returned the phone to its docking station. I walked back into the living room, picked up my coffee from the floor, and went through to the dining room to sit at the table with it, just in case mum walked in on me.

After my coffee, I went upstairs, shaved the three days worth of stubble from my face and had a nice hot shower. After drying myself, I dug out my best jeans, trainers and a polo top, and splashed on some aftershave. I felt like a man on a mission.

As I was in the kitchen preparing two cups of coffee, there was a knock at the door and then it opened.

"Honey, I'm home!" the voice bellowed.

"Go through to the dining room, Jez," I replied, "I'll be two minutes. The kettle's just boiled.

I walked through the living room into the dining room holding the two cups of hot steaming coffee, and placed them down on the coasters that Jez had already put into position. He knew the drills. I grabbed he chair opposite Jez, and as I pulled the chair out, I heard Jez's feet hit the floor with a thud.

"My mam will fucking kill you if she ever catches you with your feet on her chairs, daft lad. You know what she's like." I warned him as he pulled himself upright on his chair.

I took a few sips from my coffee, and then sat back in my chair with my arms folder across my chest.

"Right," I said, "how's about you and me going for a little cabby in your motor around Castletown?"

Jez put his cup down and stared at me for a few seconds before saying, "You sure you're ready for this mate? You not think it's a bit too soon at the moment?"

"Nah," I replied as I passed Sandra's letter to him, "read that, and you'll know why I want to find her sooner rather than later."

Jez opened the letter, and as he read it I watched his jaw drop and his head shake in disbelief. He threw the letter back at me and rubbed his brow.

"I'm sorry to say this mate, he said, "but that's bang out of fucking order. I see what you mean. Tell you what, shall we leave it until later tonight when it's a bit darker. It's just that she might see us and recognise the car if she's out and about?"

"Whatever you say, mate," I said, "sounds like a plan actually. And don't worry; I'm not looking for any trouble. I just want to find out where she lives so I can see that my boy's alright. Couldn't give a toss about her."

Jez stayed for another thirty minutes or so, then went back home for something to eat. He said he would come back at about nine o'clock that night. As soon as he left, I went back into the kitchen to make another coffee.

Just before nine o'clock, there was a knock at the front door, and the familiar voice bellowed across the hallway, "Honey, I'm home!"

Jez walked into the living room where I was sat with my mother watching the TV. He sat on the single chair opposite us.

My mother looked Jez up and down then said, "Alright Jez, son. You okay?"

"I am Mrs H, thanks." he replied with a big cheesy grin.

"Good," she continued, "well if you're staying, take your shoes off. You should know by now sunshine.

Before Jez began unlacing his shoes, I stood up and beckoned him towards the front door, and then I turned and said to mum, "Oh it's okay mam, we're not stopping. We're just popping out for a bit in his car, but we won't be long."

My mother raised her eyebrows when she looked up at me and said, "Well if you find her, don't do anything stupid. I'll help you where and when I can son, but don't go kicking off with anyone."

"Aye, no probs mam," I said as I bent down to kiss her goodbye, "we'll be good boys. I promise."

"Yes, well," she said with a grin, "if you can't be good, just don't get caught."

As we got into Jez's car, I started to explain about how we should go about our search. I suggested that we should drive to the outskirts of the area, and then walk through the centre. That way, we could quickly hide if we're spotted.

"Fucking hell, Mark," Jez mocked, "we're not on one of your covert operations, you know. You'll be asking me to wear that camouflage make up on my face next."

Jez started up the car and pulled away. It was quite a few minutes before either of us said anything else, but then Jez broke the silence.

"Anyway, what the fuck are we going to do when or if we find her tonight?" he asked.

I replied shrugging my shoulders, "Good question mate. Never really thought about that to be honest. I suppose we'll just have to cross that bridge when we come to it."

As we neared Castletown, we could see the brightly lit shopping area in front of us. Jez swung the car around, so we were facing out of town, and then parked up outside the old post office. We both got out of the car, and slowly walked towards the shopping area.

Jez looked across at me and whispered, "What if we see her in one of the shops, Mark?"

I stopped and turned to face Jez, and said, "First of all, what the fuck you whispering for? Whose on the covert mission now eh? Just act normal, and if we see her in a shop, we'll run and hide before she sees us. Now stop flapping, bitch tits."

We were in the centre of the shopping area now, and we noticed a group of youths loitering around outside a takeaway shop. When we got closer still, I indicated to Jez to go in and I followed. Jez stood against the back wall, wondering what to do next, so I just winked at him, smiled and stepped up to the counter.

"Two small kebabs with everything on, please." I said to the young assistant on the other side of the counter.

I turned around to look at Jez smiling. He was happy, because he was getting fed. I paid for the food and I handed one of the packages over to Jez. We left the shop, and walked across the road to the stone bus shelter. We sat on the cold wooden bench and tucked into our junk food.

"What's with the kebabs, mate?" Jez asked with a mouth

full of doner meat.

"Well I don't know about you Jez, but I'm fucking starving, and it's been donkey's since I've had a kebab. So I thought I'd treat us."

In between mouthfuls, Jez thanked me, and we sat there, quite content, stuffing our faces. One of the few occasions we were quiet was when we were eating.

I'd finished my kebab way before Jez, so I threw my wrapping into the corner of the bus shelter and told Jez to stay where he was and finish his food. I stood up, and slowly walked across the road towards the gang of youths outside the shop.

I randomly picked one particular lad and walked into the middle of the group to talk to him.

"Alright, mate?" I asked, "You look familiar. You're not Linda Harrison's eldest, are you?"

"No, am I fuck," he grunted, "don't even know who she is. And who the fuck are you anyway?"

I backed off with my hands in the air, just to show I wasn't after any trouble.

"Ha, sorry mate." I apologised, "Just thought we were related that's all. I seen your face when I came out of the kebab shop, and thought you looked familiar, that's all."

Harrison, you said?" one of the other youths asked as he pulled his hood down, showing his face, "there's a nice looking lass just moved into the house next door to my dad's place round the corner there in Jennifer Avenue. Got a little lad as well I think. I'm sure her name's Harrison."

I stepped back into he middle of the crowd to take a good look at the youth's face, and smiled.

"Oh really?" I said, "You got a minute?"

I put my arm around his shoulders and ushered him away from the group. We walked for about ten metres, so we were away from his friends then stopped. I reached into my pocket and pulled out some rolled up money. I handed the young lad a ten pound note, and he gave me a puzzled look.

"That's for you, son," I said to him, "and all I want you to do is to totally forget you've seen me. And I know you're going to ask, so I'll tell you. That lass next door to your dad is my ex wife, and I'm looking for her. All I need now is the house number."

The boy looked terrified, even more so with the fact that none of his friends had bothered to come down to find out what was going on. They all just stood, staring at us.

I looked up at the bewildered looking group, then back into the face of the boy stood in front of me.

"Well?" I asked, "What's the house number?"

"It's number forty six mate," he answered nervously, "you're not going to kick off, are you mister?"

I placed my hand on his shoulder and smiled to reassure him.

"Look lad, I'm not into slapping kids about. I'm just after my son, who's living in that house with my ex wife." I said, "Now like I said, if anyone asks, you've never seen me before. You understand?"

I patted him on the back and sent him on his way back to his friends, and as he ran off, he looked back and jeered, "Ha, you daft old cunt, thanks for the tenner you easy bastard!"

I looked across the road to the bus stop, and shouted for Jez. He immediately ran out across the road, resulting in the youth being trapped between the two of us. He was now stuck and couldn't get to his friends. I walked back up to him, and I could see the cockiness instantly transform back to fear.

"Listen up you little twat," I growled through gritted teeth and pointing in his face, "I know what you look like, and now I know where you live and hang out. So if I know that you're feeding me any bullshit, I'll come looking for you. And you know when I said that I'm not into hitting kids? That can soon fucking change. Now bugger off back to your little play mates and go buy yourself some sweeties or something."

I gave him a playful little slap across the back of his head as he scampered off. Jez walked towards me and asked, "What the fuck you doing, mate?"

"I've just found out where my dear beloved lives, Jez, my old mucker. Let's go and have a little look, shall we?"

We walked along past the remaining few shops, and turned right into Jennifer Avenue. It was only a short street, with bungalows on the left, and houses on the right. We continued along until we reached number forty six, paused for a fraction of a second, then continued to walk to the far end of the street. I stood and stared at Jez while I thought about what to do next. He stared back at me, not knowing what to do.

"Right," I eventually said, "let's get back to the car."

Jez looked puzzled, "Is that it? We've been told an address, and even though we don't know for sure if it's genuine, we're fucking off back home?"

"No," I replied, "Let's just get back to the car, I'll tell you when we get there."

Jez shook his head, not understanding what was going on inside my head, but he followed me anyway. We walked up the street and turned left back up past the shops towards the car. When Jez unlocked it, he got into the driver's seat, but I got into the rear passenger seat. Now he was really confused.

"All I want you to do mate," I began to explain, "is drive down to the kebab shop then let me out. When I get back in, just drive down to the bottom of Jennifer Avenue. Once we get there, you'll know what's happening."

"Dunno if I'm going to like this mind." Jez moaned as he pulled off. He turned the car around and headed down towards the shops.

As he was slowing down and about to come to a halt, I swung the door open, jumped out and grabbed the youth I spoke to earlier and dragged him onto the back seat with me.

"Don't worry son," I said to keep him calm, "I just want

my money's worth out of you."

Jez pulled away again and turned right into Jennifer Avenue. As we reached the end of the street, I instructed Jez to turn around then reverse into the dark corner by the high fence and switch the headlights off.

"Okay son," I said to the youth, "this is what you're going to do. You're going to walk up to number forty six, knock on the door as hard as you can, then sprint like fuck back to your mates round the corner. Understand?"

He looked at me and nodded nervously.

"Once you've done that," I continued, "you won't see me again. That's unless, of course, you've been filling me with shite or if you try anything funny. You know what I mean?"

Again, he just nodded at me nervously.

As I ushered him out of the car I said finally, "Go on then, get cracking. And remember, we'll be watching."

The boy got out of the car, and slowly walked up the street with his head down and his hands in his pockets. I climbed over onto the front passenger seat next to Jez, who wasn't saying a word. When the boy neared the house, I slid down my seat so my head wouldn't be visible from outside. Jez followed suit.

The boy took his right hand out of his pocket, and rapped his knuckles hard on the door. He then sprinted for his life and disappeared around the corner at the top of the street. I peered up slightly over the dashboard so I could see the house door open. A figure appeared out of the dimly lit hallway, and I could see her looking both ways up and down the street. It was Sandra, for sure. She stood at the door for a few seconds more, enough time for me to notice a cigarette in her left hand and a beer can in the other. God, she was letting herself go.

Sandra looked up and down the street once more before cursing and then slamming the door shut. Jez and I both looked at each other as we slowly sat back up in the seats.

"What now?" he asked.

"Well," I replied, "now I know where she lives, that's the main thing. I'll leave it for a day or two, and then I think I'll pay her a daytime visit. Let her know that I know. Should be an interesting conversation we have. She'll shit her knickers.

I slapped Jez on the thigh and continued, "Thank for tonight mate, I reckon I owe you a few pints for this. Tell you what, how about we drop the car off at yours, then we'll walk round to the pub, and I'll get us a few quaffs to wash that kebab down."

As Jez pulled away, he looked at me and said, "You don't have to ask me that twice. That's a damn fine idea, and it gets a big thumbs up from me."

Chapter 5

I was back in Bosnia, and I was busy carrying out a guard duty at the main gate of our barracks in Gornji Vakuf. It was night time and there was a slight chill in the air. Fog had come down from the mountains and was lying heavy on the ground, making visibility rather difficult. Gun shots could be heard in the nearby village, and the occasional car sped past the camp site along the gravelled road into the distance, but nothing to cause alarm. These sorts of things were an every day occurrence.

Holding my rifle in the "alert" position, I walked back and forth in front of the main entrance barrier. As I turned in the road to face the guard room, I noticed a figure emerging from the fog coming from the village towards me. The figure looked small and frail, and dressed in rags with a shawl over it's head to cover the face. As it moved slowly closer, I assumed it to be a woman by the bright red, but chipped, nail varnish on the end of her long spindly fingers and on the toes of her dirty bare feet. A little closer, and through the dusky light, I could see that she was carrying something in her arms close to her chest. The small bundle was sodden with blood and I could see a tiny foot handing out of one end of the bundle.

Before she came any closer, I brought my rifle up to my shoulder and looked at her through the sight. Keeping hold of my rifle with my right hand, I used my left hand to point to the ground, and ordered the woman to place her bundle down. She stopped and slowly bent downwards, placing the bundle on the ground in front of her. As she slowly rose back up she began to laugh, and when she finally stood upright, she pulled back her shawl to reveal her face. It was Sandra. Her laughing became louder and louder and then just came to an abrupt end. She looked down at the bundle as it began to roll around until the baby's face was looking at me. The blood soaked bundle was my son, Cameron.

My breathing became heavier and I could feel myself squeezing on the trigger of my rifle. Sandra stepped over the baby and walked towards me again, laughing once more. Although I warned her to stop, she continued to get closer. I held my rifle tight against my shoulder and squeezed the trigger harder, until it clicked. The end of the barrel recoiled upwards slightly as the rifle fired, and the spent round cracked out of the barrel towards Sandra.

I woke up startled from my dream, sitting up bolt upright. Cold sweat oozed from my pores and my bed sheets were drenched in urine. The stench was overwhelming. I swung my legs around and placed my feet on the floor, sitting on the edge of my bed. I looked at the alarm clock, it was only half four in the morning. My bloody alarm wasn't due to go off for another four hours. My appointment at the job centre was today, and I'm going to go there now looking like shit.

I stripped my bedding and left it in a pile by the door, then jumped into the shower to rid myself of the horrid smell of stale urine. Once I was out and dried, I put on a clean pair of shorts, and threw the soaked ones in amongst the bedding. I picked it all up, and held the bundle at arms length as I quietly crept downstairs into the kitchen, then threw it into the washing machine. It was far too early to switch it on, so I just poured some powder into the drawer and left it until later. I made myself a coffee and walked out the kitchen into the utility room leading into the garden. I sat on the wooden bench on the patio under the gazebo, and took a few sips of my coffee. My mother had left her cigarettes on the garden table, so I took one and lit it. I sat back and put my feet up on the bench. The cigarette crackled as I took a long slow drag from it, filling my lungs with its warm poison. I held my breathe for a few seconds, and then released the smoke into the air. My body began to tingle as the nicotine took effect, and I felt totally relaxed. I took another drag from the cigarette then reached over to the table for my coffee.

I listened to the bird's morning song, and watched the sun slowly climb up over the roof tops. The warmth shone against my face, and the brightness forced me to close my eyes. With the nicotine induced "high" and the warm sun against my face, I could feel myself relaxing more and I allowed myself to drift back into a deep sleep.

"What the frigging hell you doing out here, you daft sod?" mum shrieked.

I jumped up off the bench, startled, and it took a second or two before I realised where I was.

"Sorry mam," I apologised, "I just came down for some fresh air earlier, and must've just dropped off on the bench here."

My mother shook her head and continued to speak to me as if I was twelve year old, "You'll catch your death of cold out here at this time, get yourself inside, I've got the kettle on."

As I walked into the living room I looked at the wall clock, it was ten past nine. Still had plenty of time to sort myself out before going to the job centre.

My mum cam through to the dining room and placed two cups of coffee on the table.

"Come and get this down you son, it'll warm you up." she insisted.

As I walked over to the table, I smiled at her and replied, "Mam, it's not that cold out there, you know. It was quite nice actually."

She held her coffee in both hands and took a sip from it, then looked at me saying,"Oh, I've put the washing machine on for you, by the way."

I looked at her sheepishly and apologised.

She placed her cup down on the table and grabbed my hands.

"Look son, you've got nothing to be sorry for," she said, "I dread to think what's going on inside that head of yours, but either way, you need to get it sorted. I think you might need to speak to someone."

"Nah, mam," I disagreed, "once I get to see my boy then I'll be okay. I know where they live, so I'm gonna sort it. Don't worry about me; I'm a big lad now."

Mum frowned at me, and still holding tightly onto my hands she said, "You might be a man now son, but you're only human. You've been dealt with some crap lately, and you need to sort it. Speak to someone, please."

I pulled my hands away slowly and wrapped them around my cup that was in front of me, and looked up at my mother.

"I'll be okay mam; I just want to see Cameron. That's all that matters to me, you know." I said, half smiling, "When I was in the army, it was him that kept me going. He gave me something to look forward to whenever I was away. I wanted him to grow up and brag to his friends about his dad being a brave soldier. I wanted him to sit and listen to my stories. I wanted him to be proud of me, but all that's been taken away from me, mam. If I get my boy back, I can make him proud again. I can look after him. I would die for him, mam. He's my little boy."

"You know what son?" mum said, fighting back the tears "You sound so much like your dad, Mark. And if he was here now, he'd be so bloody proud of you. Despite what's happened, you need to know that you can still be proud of what you've achieved in your life. You've done what some men dream of, and they will envy you. But what you have to think about is, what would you're dad be saying to you now? He'd be telling you to get your act sorted, pull yourself together and soldier on."

I didn't give my mother any retort. I just looked at the photograph of my father on the wall behind her. It was an old black and white photograph of him that was taken by my grandfather when he passed out of basic military training as a Para. A tear rolled down my cheek as I remembered.

My father had joined the army way before I was born, and he was proud, to the point of egotism, to be a member of the elite- the Parachute Regiment. His blood wasn't red, it was maroon. Three months after returning from the Falklands conflict in 1982, he left the army after completing his full service of twenty two years. Approximately two years after his discharge, he was diagnosed with lung cancer. The disease spread at an alarming rate around his body, and it didn't take long before it took his life.

His popularity was obvious at his funeral when people were queuing outside the crematorium because of the lack of room inside. Wreaths in the form of the Parachute Regiment's emblem crammed the memorial gardens, and maroon berets could be seen everywhere. The foot of his coffin was draped with the Union Flag, and the flag of his beloved regiment was draped over the head. After the service we watched him being slowly rolled back behind the velvet curtains, where he was to be cremated. The haunting sound of bagpipes and beating drums played my father's favourite tune; Highland Cathedral, and there was not a dry eye in the house. I was only fourteen.

Even to this day, my mother remains in contact with some of dad's old army comrades. And every year she visits the crematorium where she writes a loving message in the families' book.

I remember as a young boy, sitting on my father's knee and listening to the stories he told whilst looking through his vast collection of old photos. Every photo had a story, and we would spend hours looking through them. I often fantasised about being a war hero like my dad, and would often role play with my friends, re enacting the stories he told me.

When he died, he had left me his maroon beret, his medals and all of his photos. When I joined the army though, I kept these at my mother's house for safe keeping.

I looked at my mother, she was crying too. I stood up,

walked around to her side of the table, and put my arms around her.

"Everything's going to be fine, mam," I said, "We've still got each other, and I've got loads of life in me still. So I ain't going anywhere."

She looked up at me and smiled through the tears saying, "I am proud of you son. Just don't mess things up okay? I've got you back home now, and I want you to stay."

I kissed her head and then walked back around to my side of the table to gulp down the last of my coffee.

"Right," I said, "I suppose I'd better sort myself out for this job centre bollocks. Wish me luck."

I arrived at the job centre fifteen minutes early, so I booked in for my appointment, and then walked over to the computers to carry out a job search. Although there were quite a few jobs available, the wages being offered were pathetic. I took a few printouts of some of the semi decent jobs, just to make it look like I was interested, then sat on the row of chairs to wait for my name to be called.

I was wearing a shirt and a pair of trousers, but I noticed that the majority of the other male "job seekers" were dressed in tracksuits, hooded jackets, trainers, and draped in cheap jewellery. The young women in there were no better. Did they have no personal pride? Obviously not. While I was busy people watching, I noticed a woman, who appeared to be in her mid forties, book into the reception. Her unkempt peroxide hair hung like rats tails down her head, and she appeared to have applied her thick make up with a catapult. I cringed as she walked towards the chairs and sat right next to me. She turned to me and smiled, showing off her yellow, nicotine stained teeth. She reeked of alcohol and stale tobacco, which made my stomach churn.

Within minutes, I heard my saviour call my name from a desk in the far corner. I stood up and almost sprinted towards the desk just to get away from the mutton dressed as lamb. I sat at the desk and opposite me was a young man dressed in a blue shirt and tie. His long hair was greased back and his thick black rimmed glasses covered most of his face. He definitely wasn't long out of college or university.

After punching my details into his computer, he asked for my qualifications.

"Wow," he sounded surprised but impressed, "We, hopefully, shouldn't have any problems finding you a decent job. You've got plenty of qualifications and experience to keep your options open.

"Well," I replied, "just as long as I'm not working every hour God sends for peanuts, just to line someone else's pockets."

College boy smiled at me and gave me some of his text book sympathy, "I certainly do understand, sir," he said through his false smile, "But what you need to understand is that in order to be eligible for Job Seekers' Allowance, you are required to show that you're willing to work for the national minimum wage. And you need to prove that you're actively seeking employment."

I leaned forward, resting my elbows on the desk, and glared deep into his eyes and said, "Impressive. No doubt you learned that text book phrase, with all those long words, during your training as a desk jockey. Bet you can do joined up writing as well, eh? Mammy and daddy must be really proud of their little boy. Now for the record, yes you can put down on that system of yours to say that I'm willing to work for a pittance. But if you think I'm going to stack shelves or flip burgers for the rest of my life, you're very sadly mistaken. Just put what you have to put into your computer in order to make me one of your statistics, give me whatever paperwork I need and then I'll be on my way. I don't need some *boy*, who's still sucking on his mam's tit, to tell me what I can and can't do. Fair enough?"

During the long uncomfortable silence, my eyes remained fixed on his, and his jaw just hung open. He was dumbfounded by the way I had just spoken to him. I bet he wasn't taught in college how to deal with someone like me.

After a few seconds more, he looked down at his desk and began shuffling his paperwork around whilst trying to think of what to say next. He then paused and looked back up at me, showing me his text book smile again.

"Have you ever considered self employment, sir?" he asked, feeling quite satisfied with himself that he had gotten out of a rather sticky situation.

I sat back in my chair and folder my arms across my chest, still looking into his eyes.

"Tell you what, mate," I said, "I might just look into that. If you've got any information, I'll take it off your hands, and I'll give it a good think over. To be honest, it's never really crossed my mind about going it alone, so thanks."

The boy's smile broadened, and appeared to be a genuine smile this time. He pulled open a drawer by his desk, pulled out a file, and handed me some leaflets and handouts.

"Have a look through these, sir," he informed me, "There's plenty of information and details of where you could go for possible funding and business loans."

I quickly flicked through the paperwork he had given me and then smiled back at him. As I stood up, I reached out to shake his hand. As he accepted my gesture, I could see the slight look of discomfort in his face as I took a firm grip of his perfectly manicured hand. I always believed in giving a good strong hand shake, shows strength and confidence.

I walked out of the booth, but after taking a few steps I stopped and turned round to face him again.

"By the way, son," I said, "Never call me *sir*, I worked for a living."

Chapter 6

It had been a few days since Jez and I discovered Sandra's whereabouts, and I thought it was time I personally paid her a visit and try and see Cameron.

I rang Jez to ask if he could give me a lift into Castletown, but he was at work. I didn't really want to wait until night time, because getting a visit in the dark from her "psycho" husband may freak her out. It was ten o'clock on a Saturday morning, and if my memory served me right, Cameron was an early riser, so they would both be awake. She wouldn't be able to complain about me calling at an unsociable hour. Castletown was only two miles or so away, so I decided to take the old fashioned method - on foot.

In less than half an hour I had reached the shops at Castletown, and before I turned into Jennifer Avenue, I stopped off at the small newsagent to buy a pack of cigarettes and a disposable lighter. As I walked out of the shop, I unwrapped the packet and placed a cigarette between my lips and lit it. For some reason, I was feeling quite nervous and nauseous. A lungful of smoke soon calmed me down, and I continued into Jennifer Avenue.

Once I had reached number forty six, I threw what was left of my cigarette into the drain on the side of the road, and stood in front of the door. I took a deep breathe, and then tapped on the glass partition of the door. A second or two later, I could make out a figure through the opaque glass walking towards me.

When Sandra opened the door, the colour flushed from her face instantly. Her eyes bulged and her mouth was gaping wide open.

"Pick your chin up, love. Looks like you're trying to catch flies." I said as I grinned at her.

"What the fuck are you doing here?" she asked, still bewildered.

"Well, is that the way you should be speaking to your

betrothed?" I said, "You not going to invite me in for a cuppa then?"

For some reason her expression transformed from shock to slight fear, and she stepped back to hide behind the door.

"Erm...." she stammered nervously from behind the door, "now's not a good time at the moment, Mark. You won't be able to come in right now, because erm.... Cameron's not up yet."

I took a small step back and glanced into her living room window where I could see the TV playing. I then smiled, stepped forwards towards the door and said, "Well you're either talking out of your arse, or you've taken a sudden fucking interest in the Teletubbies, sweetheart."

Sandra shook her head, now panicking, and denied, "No, I'm telling you he's in bed. He had a late night."

"In that case then," I continued, "I'll come in and wait for him to get up. I won't make a noise."

I pushed the front door wide open, pinning her behind it, and walked into the house. I stopped at the door on the left of me that lead into the living room, and there was Cameron sitting on the floor watching the TV. He had his back towards me, and I made sure not to disturb him. All I wanted to do was watch him.

The person sitting on the sofa in the corner obviously didn't notice me on the other side of the door, and he bellowed, "Who the fuck was that at the door, Sandra?"

The loudness of his voice startled Cameron, and he began to cry.

The voice now aimed itself at my son, and bellowed again, "And you can shut your fucking whining as well, you little twat!"

This made matters worse for Cameron, and he began to sob, and as I stepped into the room, Sandra came pushing through past me to get to him first.

I stood and watched Sandra as she comforted Cameron, and then I turned to face where the voice was coming from. He appeared to be in his mid to late twenties, and gave me the impression he loved himself. He lay on the sofa with his feet up, wearing only a pair of shorts, and I could see he worked out, but probably spent just as long lying under a sun bed.

"Who the fuck are you?" he shouted towards me as he bolted out of his seat.

I stepped forward, staring deep into his eyes and replied, "First of all, and more importantly; you ever speak to my son like that again, and I'll rip your fucking head off and shit down your neck. And secondly, sweetheart, you can either sit back down, or I'll knock you down."

Pretty boy had obviously realised who he had just threatened, and sat back down as quickly as he got up. I continued to stare at him for a few seconds more, letting him know he was sailing close to the wind, and then I turned my attention to Cameron.

I walked to the middle of the floor and crouched down, where Sandra was still holding him. I stuck out my hand, and Cameron looked at me. After a short pause, he smiled and grabbed my finger. He had one hell of a good grip, that's my boy! I smiled as tears of joy rolled down my face. Did he recognise me? He seemed pleased to see me, either way. I held out my other hand, invitingly, and watched his every step as he toddled towards me. As soon as he got close enough, Cameron fell into my chest. I wrapped my arms around him and gave him a huge hug, kissing his head. Before my tears became uncontrollable, I handed him back to Sandra and stood up.

"You see?" I confirmed to her, "No harm done. I just want to see my boy."

Emotionless, Sandra looked back at me and said, "Well when are you gonna start paying maintenance for him then?"

"Let me see him on a regular basis, and I'll pay my way once I've got some money coming in. And as long as the money's spent on Cameron, and not you or lover boy behind me here." I replied.

I heard the sofa behind me creak, and without even looking behind me I warned, "Sit down, sunshine. Last fucking warning."

"You're going nowhere near him on your own. You need to sort yourself out. You're not right in the fucking head!" She screamed at me, still holding onto Cameron.

"Do I need to remind you why I went off on one? In fact, does lover boy here know why we're not together any more?"

I turned to face the bronzed Adonis and ordered him to stand up.

He slowly rose from the sofa, but didn't come any closer. His steroid stuffed arms hung down by the sides of his orange torso.

"What's your name, big lad?" I asked.

"Clive" he stuttered nervously.

"Well Clive," I continued, "Did you know that your lass here is quite partial to the occasional gang bang?"

"Fuck off Mark, you bastard!" Sandra screamed again.

I turned to face her and replied, "No sweetheart, you fuck off."

As I turned back to face Clive, he was already swinging his fist towards me, striking the left side of my face. I fell back two or three paces, and before I could regain my bearings, Clive grabbed me by my jacket with both of his hands. I noticed his head coiling back slightly, preparing to head butt me, so before he got any further, I grabbed his right wrist with both of my hands. In one smooth movement, I swept my right foot behind me slightly, and using the twisting motion of his wrist and the force of my body weight spinning around and down, I brought him crashing to the floor. He was now faced downwards, chewing carpet, and his right arm was in the air, twisted into the "goose neck" position. I then slammed my left knee into his back and leaned forward, placing my body weight against his twisted hand, rendering him motionless.

My breathing became heavier and I could feel the rage gradually build up inside me. I was about to push Clive's arm further forward in order to snap his shoulder, when I realised Cameron was crying. I looked over and saw the tears streaming down his little face, and saw the look of pure terror in his eyes. I released the hold an Clive's arm and slowly stood up. I looked into Cameron's eyes and smiled, then walked out of the room. As I was opening the front door I could hear steps bounding towards me from behind, and I turned to see the bronzed Adonis storming towards me.

"Oi, fucker, I ain't finished with you yet!" he grunted as he got closer.

The second he was within reach, I took a step forward and swung my fist upwards, connecting with his chin. The punch sent him off his feet and he landed on the floor in an unconscious heap. Sandra ran out of the living room, and as I walked out of the door, I looked back and said, "Well, I did fucking warn him."

Chapter 7

Sunday night was bingo night for my mother, and as I had no plans to go out, I asked her if it was okay for the boys to come around for a few beers. She said it would be okay as long as Jez would give her and Aunt Linda a lift to the bingo hall. I rang Nick, Lurch and Jez and asked if they fancied coming here for a bite to eat and a few beers, and of course the all accepted my invitation. Jez also agreed to take mum and Aunt Linda to bingo. Sorted!

Nick and Lurch arrived together, as usual. And while we were in the kitchen stuffing the fridge with beer cans, the door opened once more and Jez shouted out his usual welcome call.

Just as I was about to call him through to the kitchen, my mother shouted down from her bedroom, "Ill not be long Jeremy son, I'm just putting my ear rings in and then I'll be down."

Nick laughed and said, "Ha, they sound like a fucking married couple, don't they?"

Both Nick and Lurch stopped and looked at me, and I stared back without any expression on my face. Then Lurch looked at Nick and said, "Thought I was supposed to be the dense twat. Nick puts his foot in it yet again. Fucking gob shite."

I suddenly broke into fits of laughter, letting them know I got the joke, and said, "Actually Nick, you've got a point there, mate."

I turned to face Jez as he was walking down the hallway towards us in the kitchen and shouted, "Hey, Jez, is there something you need to tell me? You shagging my mother?"

My mother shouted down again, "I frigging heard that, you cheeky bugger. You're not too big for a thick ear!"

Jez came into the kitchen and all four of us were giggling like little school boys. I handed them a beer each and we walked out into the garden, sitting under the gazebo. The barbecue was already fired up.

"How did it go at Sandra's yesterday then, Mark?" Jez asked.

"Well, I suppose it could've been worse, mate. I got to hold Cameron for a bit, but then I got into a bit of a scrape with Sandra's new fella."

"Fucking hell!" Lurch added, "She hasn't hung about has she?"

"Nah she hasn't," I replied, "but the jumped up little prick's welcome to her. As long as my boy doesn't come to any harm, that's all that matters."

"So who is it that she's shacked up with then?" asked Nick.

"His name's Clive, and looks like a right fucking big girl's blouse. Toned up to fuck, but punches like a bitch. Thought he was a big lad, shouting at my kid, but he nearly shat his fucking pants when he saw me walk in. Obviously, he got a bit brave while my back was turned, but if it wasn't for our Cameron, I would've snapped his fucking arm off."

Jez slammed his beer can down onto the table and exclaimed, "He was gobbing off to your boy? I'll pull his fucking foreskin over his head! That's if he's got a dick to start with."

"Ahem," mother coughed to get our attention as she stood at the back door, "Language Jeremy. Come on then son, I'm ready for bingo. We need to pick Linda up on the way."

Jez took one last sip from his beer, before getting up and pulling his car keys out of his pocket.

"Ha'way then Margie," he said with a cheeky glint in his eye, "Let's go for a spin."

"Be good boys," mother said as she waved and walked through the house to the front door.

When we heard the front door slam shut, we downed our beers, and I sent Nick to the fridge to replenish the cans.

By the time Jez returned from his taxi run, the barbecue

was well on its way and the meat was sizzling. On his way through the kitchen, Jez had grabbed four beers out of the fridge and handed them out to us.

While I stood in front of the barbecue with a spatula in one hand, a beer can in the other and a cigarette hanging out my mouth, we had our usual debate over why Lurch hasn't got a girlfriend. And as usual, it concluded with Lurch becoming wound up and Nick winding him up even further. After a few empty beer cans were thrown about the garden, we began to laugh about it. The conversation of Lurch's love life always took this form.

I carried the tray of meat over to the table where the boys were eagerly waiting to tuck in. It looked like they had starved themselves all day by the way the food was demolished within minutes.

As Lurch tucked into his belly pork, he spluttered, "You have fun at the job centre then, Mark?"

I placed my plate onto the table, took a quick sip of my beer before replying, "Oh it was fucking depressing. It was full of young jobs worth wankers behind the desks, and the so called 'job seekers' were all just alcoholics, druggies and tracksuit tramps. Apart from that, fucking champion, Lurch. Thanks for asking."

"Told you it would be a waste of time, man." Nick added, through a mouthful of burger."

"Well, actually, it wasn't a total cluster fuck. Give me a minute." I said, as I got up and went into the dining room.

I came back out carrying the paperwork I got from the job centre and placed it on the table. Jez picked it up, had a quick flick through the pages and then passed it onto Lurch.

"So you're thinking of going it alone, mate?" Jez asked.

"Aye," I replied, "I wouldn't mind it, but haven't got a fucking clue what to do."

Nick then suggested, "Well if you're a qualified fitness instructor, why don't you go for that? Fitness classes are always popular."

"Aye, go for it mate," Jez added, "stick a pair of boots and combat trousers on, call your classes 'boot camp', and you'll have the women flocking in."

Not a bad idea that, actually," I said, enthusiastically, "I might just look into that."

Lurch finished looking through the paperwork, placed it on the table and then said, "Well if you pop down to the Business Innovation Centre by the river, they can help you with everything from business plans, how to pay your own tax and national insurance, funding, setting up web sites and all sorts."

Nick and Jez looked at each other, bewildered, and then Nick turned to Lurch and mocked, "Fucking hell, Lurch. Where did you just get all that bollocks from?"

Lurch diverted his attention to Nick and said, "Fuck off Nick, you ginger twat. I'm not as thick as you look."

Apart from Lurch, we all burst into fits of laughter. Lurch may give out the impression that he's not the sharpest tool in the box, but he has his intellectual moments. And his sense of humour and one liners were rib cracking.

I leaned across the table and ruffled Lurch's hair saying, "You're a fucking cracker, mate."

Still unimpressed and sulking, Lurch murmured, "Aye, but he's still a gobby ginger twat. He takes the piss out of me while he sits there stinking of fox's piss."

That last comment didn't really help with Lurch's bad mood, because we were laughing even harder. I almost wet my pants, and Jez fell backwards off his chair.

Lurch stood up and walked off into the house. Seconds later, he came back with four more beers. He placed two on the table in front of me and Jez then threw another into Nick's lap. He sat down, opened his beer, and guzzled half of the contents before placing it onto the table and let out an enormous burp.

"Anyway, Mark," he continued, "If you need a hand with anything, just give me a shout, mate."

"Ta, Lurch," I thanked him, "I'll bear you in mind. And if any of you get any more brain waves, send them my way."

Nick shot out of his chair, stood to attention and saluted, shouting, "Sir, yes sir!"

Lurch shook his head in embarrassment and said to Nick, "Sit down you ginger fuck."

Chapter 8

As I struggled through the baking hot desert sand, the sun showed no mercy by beating its searing rays down on me. There was nothing but sand for miles, and without a cloud in the sky, there was no where to hide from the heat.

My sweaty palms struggled to hold onto my rifle, and my shoulders ached from the weight in my rucksack. It felt like I had been walking for ever.

I had reached a steep sand dune, and had no choice but to climb it. I strapped my rifle tight against my chest in order to be able to have my hands free, should the need arise. I leaned forward, and dug into the sand, and powered up the soft powdery incline. It felt like I was getting nowhere, as the sand was so soft, I was slipping back slightly with every step. After a minute or two of climbing, I looked up and realised that I wasn't even half way up. The incline was becoming steeper, so I dropped to my knees and crawled the rest of the way to the peak. Just as I reached the peak, I collapsed on to my belly with exhaustion, my face buried into the sand. The weight of the rucksack pinned me to the ground, so I undid the straps around my arms and rolled the cumbersome weight of me. My shoulders and back throbbed with the relief of the weight being removed, and I felt like I was being lifted. Despite the sand being soft, my rucksack instantly rolled back down the dune, and I did not have the energy to catch it before it was too late.

I rolled over onto my back, and undid the rifle sling, and carefully placed it by my side. Then I popped the chin strap of my helmet, and as soon as I took it off my head, I felt a cool rush as my sweaty head was finally exposed to the elements.

The peak of the sand dune was almost within my reach, so I rolled onto my front and crawled the last few paces to the top. My heart sank as I could see nothing but more sand as far as the eye could see. My face dropped into the sand.

Where was I? Why am I alone, and how did I get here? All I wanted to do was go home to my family, but I didn't know which way to go. I was lost.

The cool breeze on my head was slowly becoming stronger, and when I looked up, I could see a large grey cloud in the far distance, moving rapidly in my direction. As it got closer, the wind was getting stronger and stronger. I watched the cloud swirling towards me, and the closer it got, the more ferocious the wind became. Sand was now being tossed into the air, making vision almost non existent. I turned onto my back and just as I stood to run down the sand dune, the wind caught me, and sent me hurling down the hill. I rolled all the way down to the foot of the dune, and I curled myself into a ball with the intention of protecting myself from the sand storm.

The storm went just as quickly as it arrived, but I was almost buried in the drift. I dug myself out, and stood up to brush away the sand from my face. To the left of me, I could make out one of the straps of my rucksack, so I pulled it out of the sand, and sat next to it. I unzipped one of the side pouches, and removed the water bottle for a drink. It was empty! In despair, I threw myself onto my back and looked up into the clear sky. What the hell was going on? I just lay there, not knowing what to do.

Back over the other side of the dune, I could hear a faint whirring sound, and it was quickly getting louder, building into a roar. I looked up and saw a Chinook helicopter rise over the sand dune, and it hovered above me. The twin blades threw sand into the air, and I shielded my eyes as I watched the rear hatch of the craft drop open. Although I could not see anyone stood there, I saw a rope being dropped down towards me, and the helicopter manoeuvred downwards closer to me.

Leaving my rucksack, helmet and rifle, I decided to climb the rope. This was my opportunity to get to safety. As I climbed, the helicopter began to move forward and upwards. The further up the rope I climbed, the higher the helicopter flew, and by the time I was half way up, I must have been at least one hundred feet up in the air. My heart pounded with the fear of falling, but this made me climb faster to safety. Just as I was about to reach the end and almost touching the helicopter platform, I saw a pair of boots standing there. I looked up, and there stood Sandra in military uniform. She stared at me and watched me struggling to hold on. I managed to get hold of the platform edge, and I was now hanging on to the end of the helicopter as it climbed higher into the clouds. Sandra squatted down to get a closer look at me, and she began to laugh as she noticed the look of sheer terror in my face.

Sandra stood back up, and looked to her left, beckoning someone or something. Cameron came forward and stood by her side and he was also dressed in military combats. He stood there and outstretched his arms towards me and began crying, but there was no sound coming from his mouth. As she continued laughing, Sandra stood behind Cameron, and placed her hands on his shoulders.

The laughing came to an abrupt end, and the emotion suddenly disappeared from Sandra's face. Tilting her head to one side, she looked at me and said, "You've got a choice, Sergeant Harrison. Save yourself and climb in, or save the child."

"What do you mean?" I screamed at her.

Without answering, Sandra began laughing again, and shoved Cameron forwards, and he tumbled off the edge of the platform into the abyss.

"No!" I yelled.

I let go of the platform and dropped at a rapid rate of knots. I was falling backwards, so I turned myself around until I was facing downwards. I could see Cameron below me, screaming for me and holding out his hands. We were both falling fast, but I was catching him. In order to make my body shape more aerodynamic, I stiffened my legs and kept my feet together, and held my arms into the sides. I was swiftly closing up on Cameron, and I was soon touching his fingertips with mine. Just another few millimetres and I would have him.

The sky suddenly became dark, and was almost pitch black. Simultaneously, Cameron's fall was accelerating, and was soon out of reach. The further he got away, the more difficult it became to see him, and he soon disappeared into the darkness. I screamed for him, but my voice was muted

I was falling into a black nothingness and there was no sign of the ground getting any closer. I couldn't see a thing.

"You fucked up again, Mark," Sandra's voice boomed from nowhere. "You're going to die, Mark."

Instantaneously, the sky became bright again, and the sun was blinding. I shielded my eyes until my eyesight readjusted to the intense light. I removed my hands from my eyes, and my heart almost stopped with the shock of the ground being almost upon me. This was it; I really was going to die. I felt my whole body tense up as I braced myself for the impact. Just as I was about to hit the floor, everything went blank again.

I was rudely awoken from my dream by my mother who was shouting up the stairs for me to get my sorry arse out if bed to tidy up the mess we had all left last night. I didn't have a clue what she was on about. It actually took a few seconds for me to register where I was, because a few moments ago, I was hanging out the back of a bloody helicopter. These dreams were getting more weird by the day. I sat up and was pleased that I was only soaked in sweat this time, rather than urine.

I gave myself a shake to bring me back into reality, and as I stood up, my body reminded me that I'd had quite a heavy night of drinking. The room began to spin and my stomach churned. That horrible gut feeling rose up to my throat, and it felt like I was about to vomit. I sat back down again in order to regain myself.

After a few more minutes, I decided to drag myself downstairs, slowly though. When I looked out the kitchen window into the back garden, I realised what my mother was on about. It was obvious that the beer monster had paid me a visit, and it had totally trashed the back garden, kicked my head about like a football, hen left a huge shit in my mouth. I felt like death warmed up.

"Oh my God, what a sight!" moaned mother as she saw me stood at the window, with my eyes looking like piss holes in the snow, and my hand down my shorts scratching my balls.

"I think you need to sort yourself out lad, and then sort my bloody garden out. Well, what's left of it, anyway." She barked, walking into the living room.

"Aye mam," I whinged as I followed her, "just give me a few minutes to pull myself together. I feel rotten."

"I'm surprised you're still alive," she went on, "after the amount of bloody alcohol you lot put away last night."

I protested, "Erm….. I only had a few cans, mam."

"Did you bollocks!" she scorned, "You finished all of your beers, and then you raided my drinks cabinet. You've necked all my frigging brandy and sherry!"

"Ah, that'll explain why I feel like shit then." I said as I sank into the sofa.

"Yes," she went on, "and I suggest you start feeling a lot better, and sharpish, because if you think I'm tidying up all that mess outside, you're sadly mistaken."

"Yes mam, I'll sort it." I said sheepishly.

I slowly got back up off the sofa, and paused while I waited for my head to stop spinning. Then I slowly shuffled myself back upstairs and climbed into the shower, hoping that it would put some life back into me.

My mother had gone out while I was in the shower, so when I went back downstairs I made myself a cup of strong coffee and sat at the dining table. My head still pounded and my stomach was churning and as I stared into my coffee cup, I tried to make sense of the dream. It just didn't add up.

Once I downed the dregs of my coffee, I walked through the kitchen and out the back door into the garden. One leg of the gazebo was bent inwards causing it to lean down at one corner. Beers cans and cigarette butts were strewn all over the lawn, and there were remnants of burgers and steaks left to go stale on the barbecue How the bloody hell did it get in this state? I couldn't remember a thing.

I went back into the kitchen to grab some bin liners and a sweeping brush, and then went back into the garden to clear up my mess. I filled four bags with empty cans, bottles, cigarettes and cold stale meat, and I even managed to straighten the gazebo leg enough so that mother wouldn't notice it. Her eyesight wasn't at it's best these days. Once my clear up was complete, I trundled back into the house and made myself another strong coffee to help clear my head.

My eyes were beginning to feel heavy and I could feel myself dozing off on the sofa, when there was a knock at the door. I sighed heavily, got up off the sofa and shuffled to the front door. As I was only wearing a pair of shorts, I partially opened the door and peered my head around it. There stood Sandra.

"I've got something for you." she said as she fumbled around in her handbag.

As she searched, my attention was diverted to my old car parked on the roadside. The bronzed Adonis was sat in the front passenger seat and Cameron was in the back, strapped into his booster cushion.

My attention then darted back to Sandra when she handed me a large brown envelope.

"There you go," she said, "that's for you from my solicitor."

"So what is it?" I asked as I opened it. "Seems like there's all sorts in here."

She stood there with her arms folded across her chest, looking defiant, and said, "It's a letter from my solicitor to tell you that I'm filing for divorce on the grounds of unreasonable behaviour, and that I want an injunction taken out against you, so you can come nowhere near me or Cameron."

Before I had the opportunity to give her any feedback, she walked off towards the car. As she closed the gate behind her, she turned back to me and suggested, "Oh, and by the way, you might want to brush your teeth or something, because you fucking stink of booze."

She climbed into the car and sped off, not giving me any chance to retaliate.

"Just what I fucking need." I muttered to myself as I shut the door and walked back into the living room.

As well as having a banging head ache and a churning stomach, the letter from Sandra had placed me in an even worse mood and didn't feel like going anywhere or doing anything today. So I made myself another coffee and went up stairs to get dressed, before mother came back.

Once I was ready, I sat by the computer in the spare room and took a note pad out of the desk drawer. While the computer was booting up, I made a few notes about what I would need to start up fitness classes. I used the internet to price up equipment, and I visited several estate agents' websites to enquire about commercial property letting. There were quite a few small industrial units available in the area, and were actually reasonable priced. All I needed was a building with enough space to carry out group fitness training for approximately thirty people, enough storage space for all my equipment, and a small office.

Although I've got some money put away for that "rainy day", I made several phone calls enquiring about the possibility of funding and grants. I spoke to a cheery sounding man called Steve who worked for a company called "Business Direct". They are a company who specialise in giving advice to those aiming to go into self employment.

Steve appeared to be quite keen about my idea when I

gave him my intentions, and insisted that I paid him a visit at three o'clock. As this would give me plenty of time to sober up and pull myself together, I agreed to meet up for an informal interview. Despite the fact that I didn't have a clue where to start looking, I made a few more notes to make it look otherwise.

"Business Direct" was a small office on the outskirts of the city centre that had three people running it. There was a desk either side of the room, each of them a nerve centre of business, with telephones ringing and computers spewing out mountains of information for potential business owners. A woman sat on the left hand desk interviewing a man who sounded like he knew less than me when it comes to running a business. The woman on the right hand desk was busy talking on the telephone to someone about retaking GCSE exams. At the back of the room was an open door leading into what appeared to be a private interview room. As I entered the office a tall skinny man walked out of the back room towards me, offering his hand for me to shake.

"Hi there," he welcomed me in quite a jolly manner, "I'm Steve. Can I help you?"

I shook his hand and replied, "Yes mate, I'm Mark Harrison. I spoke to you earlier today about my ideas for setting up my own fitness classes."

His eyes instantly lit up as he remembered, "Ah yes, army man, isn't it? Come through to the back room and let's have a chat."

I followed him through to the back room, and he offered me a seat by his desk. Even before I was seated, Steve was ready with his notepad and pen.

"Right then, Mark," he began, "let's start about you telling me about yourself, and what it is you want to do. Then we'll go from there."

The next twenty minutes or so was spent with me giving my whole army history, apart from what happened with the court martial. Steve just sat and listened, totally enthralled and occasionally scribbling down notes. I then went on to explain what qualifications I have and my ideas about running a military style fitness boot camp.

Steve seemed rather excited about my idea, telling me that it has potential to be very successful. I could almost hear his mind working overtime, wondering where he could begin to help me. He was keen, very keen indeed.

Once I had given Steve all the information he required, he placed his pen carefully on the desk, sat back in his chair, and finally relaxed.

"Right," he said, "What we need to do first is put a business plan together. But don't worry; we can sort that out for you.

"Oh, thank God for that," I said relieved, "My mate mentioned business plans, and I didn't have a clue what he was harping on about."

"Well, like I said," he continued, "The business plan is put together just so that we can put your ideas forward to a panel who decide whether or not it's worth plying money into it, and if so, how much."

I leaned forward and asked Steve, "So how much do you reckon I'd be able to get?"

"First of all," Steve answered, "You have to show that you're able to provide some of your own funding towards the business. As far as the funding we provide is concerned, you could possibly get about two thousand quid, give or take. But what happens is, you tell us what equipment you require and how much it all costs, which you've done already. Then we go and physically go and buy the stuff for you, rather than giving you the cash."

"That sounds good to me." I said feeling rather confident and satisfied.

"Okay then. Mark," he continued, "Just leave it with me,

and I will get the ball rolling, as they say. I'll give you a tinkle if I need anything else from you, but there shouldn't be any dramas. The whole thing should take about two weeks, so hopefully, if all goes well. I will be contacting you in a couple of weeks with some good news. In the meantime, find somewhere to carry out your business, and if you need any more help, you know where I am."

I stood up and shook Steve's hand firmly. I could feel myself subconsciously grinning from ear to ear. I felt really confident about this, and if I put my mind to it, it could really be the making of me. At least it's given me something positive to focus on.

Within four weeks, my business plan had been accepted and the equipment had been purchased. I had spent two solid weeks decorating and furnishing the unit so it was exactly the way I wanted it.

The front door of the building lead into a small corridor, which was painted top to bottom in olive green and matt black. The walls were also covered in military photos and posters. At the end of the corridor was my booking office which was decorated in a similar fashion to the corridor. To the right of the office was the door leading into the main training area. The whole room had padded flooring, and every wall was mirrored. To the rear of the building was another door leading into the changing area, where customers could safely leave their personal belongings in lockers, and could also take a shower after a training session. My equipment, such as medicine balls, boxing gloves and pads, skipping ropes, aerobic steps and hand weights were strategically placed around the outside edges of the training room.

Adapting the unit to my needs and ideas took a lot of hard work, and I wouldn't have been able to manage if it wasn't for my family and friends. So to show my appreciation, I gave them all life time membership to my club. Somehow though, I couldn't imagine my mother coming to use the facilities.

My opening day was a huge success, and within less than

twelve hours, I received more than three hundred membership applications. Advertising through the local paper and the radio certainly paid off. Jez's car had also gained a considerable amount of mileage during the last few weeks as we toured the city doing leaflet drops.

My boot camp had become an overnight success, and was extremely popular with the ladies. Jez was definitely right, the combat trousers and boots certainly did the trick. It was only a matter of weeks before the workload rapidly increased, and there was no signs of it easing off, so I hired someone to act as my assistant, and carry out all of the administrative tasks in order to allow me to get on with more lessons.

Lucy was an intelligent young woman who hadn't long left college. She had studies IT skills and what she didn't know about computers wasn't worth knowing. Her telephone manner was spot on and she as great with the customers. Lucy had a great head for figures, so she was also a great help with my accounting. Despite having very little experience, she as a God send. Her boyfriend was in the RAF, but we all have our faults.

It felt like life was just starting to get back on track, and it felt good. I had something positive to focus on, and I was loving my work.

Chapter 9

It was a Sunday morning and I was up and dressed by six o'clock, ready to take my surprisingly popular "early birds" session at work. The van's fuel gauge was indicating low, so I decided to divert to the bank to draw out some money for fuel.

I parked directly outside the bank, and as I walked towards the cash machine, I noticed that down the side of the building in the alleyway, sat two men against the wall. They were smoking and drinking, and looked worse for wear. They were either starting extremely early, or they were still carrying on from last night. Either way, they were shit faced. As I stood at the cash machine, I cold hear their voices becoming gradually louder as they came out of the alleyway and stood behind me, waiting to use the cash machine.

The men were whispering between themselves, and as I pushed my card into the dispenser, and punched in my four digit number, I could feel them getting closer up behind me.

"Oi, mate," one of them slurred to me, "any chance of a few quid?"

I pressed the "cancel" button, pulled the card out, and quickly placed it into my jacket pocket before turning round to face them.

"Sorry lads," I replied, "I've only got enough cash to fill my van up until I get paid on Friday."

The man on my right put his hand in his jacket pocket while he took a few more steps closer towards me, and pulled out a small knife and pointed it at me.

I turned ninety degrees so my back was no longer against the wall, and I took a few steps back to give me more space between us.

"I don't think you're understanding us, mate," the

knifeman threatened, "we want your money, and you're gonna fucking give us it."

My eyes never left the knife, and as I put my hands in the air, I said to them both, "Look lads, waving a knife about at people isn't going to get you anywhere, apart from prison or hospital. So why don't you just drop it, and we'll forget about this ever happening."

"The only cunt going into hospital will be you if you don't stick your fucking car back in that machine and give us some money!" The knifeman said, getting closer and more agitated.

"Tell you what then lads, "I said, "The card's here in my jacket pocket. If you can get it out, you can help yourself. In fact, I'll even give you the fucking pin number!"

By now, I felt more agitated than the two drunken thugs facing me. Who the fuck do they think they are? I was daring them to come and get me.

As I positioned myself in a fighting stance, I urged them to make the first move, "Come on then! If you've got the fucking balls, come and get it."

My fists were clenched so tightly, my knuckles were almost bursting through the skin.

The knifeman lunged forward, and I quickly stepped aside. I grabbed his wrist with my right hand, and then I slammed the palm of my left hand into the back of his elbow. The cracking sound was almost sickening as I snapped his arm. He screamed in agony and as he crouched down to nurse his broken arm; I slammed my fist in a hammer motion onto the back of his head, knocking him to the floor. He was now out cold.

Just as I looked up towards the other man, I felt his left fist jab me square in the face, which was the followed by a right hook to my cheek. I was dazed slightly and lost my footing for a second or two, which was more than enough opportunity for the man to get me into a head lock. As his left arm kept a tight strangle hold around my neck, his right fist repeatedly pounded into my face, and I was rapidly loosing consciousness. I had to act quickly. In one swift movement, I grabbed the back of his left knee with my left hand, and my right arm came over the back of his head landing my hand on his chin. I lifted his knee upwards and his chin backwards, and his gripped soon loosened off my neck as he lost his balance and fell backwards. I continued the motion until I was stood upright, and he landed flat on his back, knocking the wind out of him. Once he was on he floor, I stood bent over, trying to catch my breathe, but he was soon rolling over onto all fours trying to get back up. Before he had the chance to get back onto his feet, I stepped to his side, and swept my right foot upwards into his rib cage, sending him crashing back to the ground.

I ran back over to my van and locked myself inside. As I grabbed my mobile phone, I noticed the two men crawling about on the floor, not really knowing where they were or what had just happened. The policeman who answered my call was confused when I told him that I had been attacked. He couldn't understand the fact that two men had just attacked me, one of them with a knife, and I was ringing to report it. I don't think it quite sunk in with the policeman that I got the better of them, and they were worse of than me. After explaining the situation over and over, the policeman eventually asked me for my location, and informed me that he would be sending a patrol car.

I sat in the van, and lit a cigarette. The second the smoke entered my lungs I could feel my body tingle and relax, despite having a throbbing headache. The two men were now on their feet, but still disorientated. Hopefully, the police will be here before it's too late, because I don't think I've got the energy to do any more.

The patrol car came speeding around the corner, and I let out a huge sigh of relief as it screeched to a halt. The two policemen left the car, and as one cautiously approached the two dazed men, the other walked over to my van and tapped on the window.

"Are you Mark Harrison, sir?" he asked as I wound my window down.

"I certainly am mate," I replied, "and those are the two tossers who tried mugging me."

I then shouted over to the other policeman, warning him that one of those men had a knife on him.

"Are you okay, Mark?" the policeman asked, "You look a bit battered and bruised. Did you lose consciousness at all?"

"I nearly did, but I managed to get him off me in time." I replied.

As I was explaining to the policeman what had actually happened, I kept a close eye on his comrade who was busy handcuffing the two assailants. The two drunkards were no longer putting up a fight. One by one, they were escorted into the back of the police car, then the policeman cam over to join his partner.

"Right," he informed me, "that's those two toe rags arrested and packed away. They'll be coming back to the station with us for questioning. We will, however, require a statement from you at some point, so is there any chance we can have your contact details please?"

I reached into my sports bag in the front passenger foot well, and pulled out one of my business cards.

"There you go mate," I said as I handed him the card, "All my contact details are on there. Just give me a bell, and I'll come down as soon as I can."

The policeman studied the card and then smiled, "Ah, I've heard about you," he said, "You're that ex soldier who's doing those boot camp things aren't you?"

"Yes I am mate," I replied, "Tell you what, if you ever pop down I might give you some discount. Not that I'm saying you need it mind. In fact, if you manage to get those two twats in your car locked away, I'll even throw in a few freebie lessons."

The policeman laughed, "I'll bare that in mind Mark. In

the meantime, you'll be expecting a call from us soon."

Both of them walked over to their car, and were gone as quickly as they arrived. I sat in the van, and the whole incident was now sinking in. Slowly but surely, it dawned on me that I could've been lying in a pool of my own blood, bleeding to death from a stab wound. All for the sake of a few quid. Should I have just given them the money, and then reported the robbery afterwards? Would they have attacked me regardless? The rage and frustration were flowing through my mind as I thought of those two men having the audacity to demand money and threaten me. Who are they to point a fucking knife at me? What is it with people these days, being so damn disrespectful, ignorant and selfish? Does no one know the meaning of respect these days?

I lit up another cigarette and took a few long heavy drags from it, and then it dawned on me. The policemen had just buggered off and left me battered and bruised. I could have concussion, and I'm just about to drive. Bet the police are waiting around the corner for me, so they can pull me for being unfit to drive. Now that would be a result for them, three arrests in a matter of minutes.

Apart from the banging headache, I was feeling extremely fed up. I just could not get over what had happened. Those two drunken yobs will probably end up with a slapped wrist and told not to do it again.

I looked at the clock on my dashboard; it was ten minutes to seven. I took one last drag from my cigarette, and then threw the butt out of the van window. With the window still wound down, I drove off to work. The police were nowhere in sight.

When I arrived at work, I locked up the van and pulled up the shutters to the "Sweat Box". As I walked along the corridor I hit the light switch, and the fluorescent tubes flickered on, worsening my headache, and forcing me to clamp my eyes tight shut. I opened the office door, flicked the window shutter switch, and as the shutter rose, the light shimmering through almost blinded me. My head was simmering on boiling point, and felt like it was about to explode, and I began to feel slightly dizzy. Before my legs had the chance to give way beneath me, I sat on the office chair, and put my feet up on the desk. I rested my head on the back of the chair as the room began to spin, and there was a high pitched humming in my ears. My neck was struggling to support the weight of my head, and I was feeling very tired. It felt like there was a hand on the back of my head pushing it downwards, urging me to sleep. I moved my feet from off the desk, placed my hands in front of me, and rested my head on my hands. I felt so bloody tired and weak.

I awoke as I was being strapped into the stretcher and an oxygen mask being placed over my face. There were people stood around me, but everything was a blur, and I was totally oblivious to which voice belonged to which person. I was wheeled out of the unit and into the back of the ambulance where a paramedic sat with me, carrying out his observations whilst the driver sped off to the hospital.

My faculties eventually came back to me while I was in the hospital bed, but my head was still pounding. Jez and Lurch were sat on one side of the bed, while my mother was sat on the other, holding my hand.

I sat up in my bed and panicked, "Shit! Who's at the unit?"

"It's alright son," my mum assured me, "Nick's down there now. He said he was going to hang around for another hour or so, then lock up and put the keys through our letterbox at home. So don't worry."

I sighed with relief and lay back down. I turned to Jez and Lurch and asked if they were okay.

"Sod us, man," Jez said, "What the frigging hell you doing scrapping with two blokes? One of them had a knife as well, for fuck's sake!"

I sat back up in my bed and frowned as I responded, "The cheeky twats were trying to mug me, mate. Would you just hand your money over to two drunken scumbags?"

It was Lurch's turn to talk, "Well I'm sorry mate, but if someone was pointing a knife at me, I'd be giving them the money. It's just not worth the risk. You probably could've just given them a tenner or something to get rid of them."

"Nah!" I disagreed, "I'm not letting anyone treat me like shit, and threaten me. I will put up a fight with any scum like that."

I turned to my mother as she said, "Well you've been bloody lucky, son."

I could feel myself becoming all worked up again, and my blood pressure was slowly rising as the anger returned.

"You don't understand, mam," I said through gritted teeth, "Why should I give anything to anyone that shows no respect. I would never speak to or threaten anyone like that, especially just for a few quid. If anyone gives me shit, they should expect to have it thrown back in their faces, but twice as fucking hard."

The tears were now rolling down mum's face and I grabbed her hand to reassure her, "Look mam, I know you worry, but I'll b okay. I'm just struggling with people at the moment. I don't like the way people treat each other.

"Mark, son," mum continued, "You're my only child and I'm not going to lose you. Get yourself sorted, whatever it takes. When you get out of here, speak to someone, before it's too late."

Jez agreed with my mother, "Aye mate, I think you need to see someone. You're not the same Mark I used to know."

My head spun to face Jez, "Not the same? I fucking know I'm not the same as I used to be because I've been brought up properly and been taught the meaning of respect and I've been taught how to be loyal and how to treat people right. Maybe some people round here need to fucking learn some respect themselves!"

Lurch stood up and patted me on the shoulder as he spoke to Jez, "Come on mate, think it's time we gave him some peace and quiet. Mark needs to rest, and I think it's times to leave.

Before they left, Jez and Lurch gave my mother a hug and then waved at me as they walked out of the room.

My mother's tears continued to roll as she looked at me and said, "Think you might have been a bit harsh there mind, darling."

"Well," I replied defiantly, "what they fuck do they know?"

Mum stood up at the side of my bed, and she took a firm grip of my hand.

"I'll put it down to you not being well, son. But don't ever speak to me like that again. I love you with all my heart, but you seriously need help. I'm going home now, because I think you need some rest. I'll pop back over tomorrow."

After kissing me on my forehead, mum picked up her handbag and walked out without saying another word or looking back. That was her way of letting me know I'd pissed her off. I lay back in my bed, grab the remote control for the portable television and switched it on to watch the mindless daytime programmes being broadcasted. I often wondered why so many people complained about the price of a TV licence, but now I know why. What a crock of shit!

The five days in hospital were mind numbingly boring, and I was itching to get back home. Not to see my family and friends, but to get back to work. I needed to get back into focus. My mother ordered me to stay put when I attempted to discharge myself after three days, and I thought that after the way I had previously spoken to her, it would be best to obey.

Jez was good enough to come and pick me up from the hospital, and while we were in the car, I apologised for the way I spoke to him the other day.

"Nah," he said, "Don't worry about it. You're going through a load of shit, mate. I know it wasn't anything personal. We're all just worried about you that's all."

I felt good knowing that my mates were around me, and no matter how much earache I gave them, they came back for more. Jez was like a loyal puppy. It's just a shame that the rest of society couldn't take a few leaves out of his book.

I was meant to spend three weeks relaxing, but after a week of my mother's constant fussing, I needed to get out. As much as I love my mother, she was doing my head in. I couldn't even take a shit without her wanting to wipe my arse.

Despite being advised otherwise, I drove the van to work, and opened up the unit. It felt like I'd never been away. After switching all the lights on I returned to the office, switched the kettle on and looked about the office. The place was spotless and still well organised. While I had been in hospital, Lucy held the fort and kept the place running. She had even organised for an old army mate of mine to come in and carry on with the lessons, in order to keep my customers.

I leaned back in the office chair and put my feet up on my desk, and as I sipped my coffee I heard the front door swing open, and the familiar "click click" of high heeled shoes scurrying down the corridor towards the office. Lucy flew into the office and hurled herself at me, throwing her arms around me and smothering me in kisses. For some strange reason, I had just a small inkling that she was pleased to see me.

"It's a bloody good job your lad's away, innit?" I said in between kisses and hugs, "He'd blow his frigging top if he saw you throwing yourself all over me."

"Ah, bugger him," she replied, "As long as you're okay, that's the main thing. It's been crap here without you, just glad to have you back in the hot seat.

Once she had calmed down and straightened herself out, she sat at her desk and switched on her computer.

"Right," she said, "it's nice to have you back, but you've got a lesson in half an hour. Twenty four women wanting you to get them all hot and sweaty. So you better get yourself ready and set up. When they start coming in, I'll do my usual and send them through to the changing rooms."

"Jesus Christ, lass," I exclaimed, "You don't hang around do you? I best get a shifty on."

I reached over her desk, and gave Lucy a peck on her cheek, and went over to the changing rooms to prepare myself. As I was setting up for the lesson, some of the ladies had started to arrive, so I asked them to wait in the changing rooms until I was done and until everyone had arrived. Once I had set up, I checked with Lucy to see if everyone was present, and she informed me that only two people were missing.

I entered the exercise room and shouted, "Right girls, get yourselves out here, and let's get cracking!"

The women came out of the dressing room in dribs and drabs, looking terrified. I smiled and ushered them to the benches in the briefing area. As the last few ladies made themselves comfortable, I began my usual introductory chat.

I stood in front of them and began, "Good morning ladies, I'm Mark, and today, I'm going to make you ache in places you've never ached before. You have never experienced a fitness session like the one you're going to get today, and you will never forget it. As most of you may already know, I am an ex soldier and physical training instructor, and my lessons are designed to help improve your overall fitness and even lose some weight. I carry out these lessons exactly the same way I used to carry out military lessons. I expect nothing but maximum effort from all of you, and I haven't got time for wasters. There's no such thing as 'can't', and you will work hard for me. If you enjoy today, and you intend to come back for more lessons, you will soon reap the benefits and will notice the difference in your fitness. You will feel better within yourself, although you might not be thinking that within the next half hour or so. Have any of you got any questions?"

Not a peep. The women just sat there, mouths gawping wide open and shaking their heads. I went on to explain and demonstrate the exercises I had set up for them, and then I got them onto the floor and gave them a fitness sessions to remember. Within ten minutes, sweat was pouring from every one of them, and I made sure that I got one hundred per cent from them all. They worked damn hard.

An hour later, the women were in the changing rooms, and I was in the office sipping the hot fresh coffee that Lucy had just made for me. Half an hour later, the women came out of the changing rooms crossed over the exercise room and passed the office. Despite the fact that they had just received an hour long thrashing, each and every one of them thanked me as they left. Whether or not the thanks was sincere didn't matter, I was satisfied. I felt at home again.

No more lessons were booked in for the rest of the day, Lucy wanted to break me back in gently I think. I told Lucy that she could go home early as she deserved it. I think what really made her day was the pay rise I told her I was giving her. I believe that people should be recognised for their loyalty and hard work.

As I was about to switch all the lights off to lock up, the telephone began to ring. When I answered it, a hoarse gravely voiced man introduced himself.

"Hello there am I speaking to the business proprietor?" the man asked.

"Yes I'm Mister Harrison, I run the place. How can I hep you?" I replied.

"Well hello there Mister Harrison," the voice continued, "I'm Eric Barnes of Epic Security Company, and I am ring you to offer you some help. Businesses like yours may, every now and again, come across certain problems that your unable to sort out yourself. Now and again people may enter your premises who may be a bit erm...unsavoury, shall we say? And these are the kind of people who can make your life ever so uncomfortable, if you know what I mean. We are the people who can protect you and your company from these such problems and unruly people. For a weekly fee, we can have our personnel on permanent stand by, waiting to be of assistance to you."

"Thank you for your offer Mister Barnes," I said as I rolled my eyes, "But I'm doing fine as I am. I won't be requiring your business offer."

There was a slight pause before the voice persisted, "Mister Harrison, we are a popular company within the Sunderland area where many businesses have joined us for our services. It really would be in your best interests to use our protection, as you never know what's around the corner. Tell you what I'll do, within the next day or two, I'll send a couple of my staff around to have a little chat with you. Maybe they will be able to explain more clearly why you should use our company."

"Well I am a busy man," I added, "But if I'm free when they come here, I'm more than willing to have a natter with your blokes. Right Eric, it's been nice chatting to you and all that, but I must dash now, I've got a busy day ahead of me and I need to get cracking."

Before Eric could reply, I hung up. I didn't have the time to listen to a cowboy businessman trying to sell me a con.

While I was locking up the unit, I came to the decision that I was doing well enough financially to start paying towards the upkeep of my son. The last thing I wanted was for Sandra to have an opportunity to make Cameron think I didn't care or do my part. I started up the van and made my way to Castletown.

Muscle brain answered the door, and let me through to the living room. Cameron was having an afternoon nap on the sofa, and Sandra was sat by him watching crappy daytime television.

"How the fuck can you watch that shite?" I asked, laughing.

Without even acknowledging my joviality, Sandra looked

up at me and asked, "Can I help you?"

Realising she wasn't too pleased to see me; I straightened my face and replied to her straight-to-the-point question, "Well I just thought I'd pop in to sort out some sort of arrangement with you for Cameron's maintenance. But if you're not interested....."

A smile suddenly appeared on Sandra's face, as I predicted would have happened with the sound of money. And she was now giving me her full attention.

"Will a hundred quid a week be enough for him?" I asked, already knowing the answer.

Sandra's face lit up as she replied, "God aye! More than enough Mark."

"Well I thought you'd be pleased with that, "I added, "But note what I said; the money's for Cameron. Not you. If I find out that you're pissing my money up the wall, or spending it on anything else but Cameron, Then you'll get fuck all else from me. You understand?"

Sandra nodded.

"And there's one more condition," I went on; "You speak to your solicitor, and drop this injunction bollocks."

"Well it seems like you're starting to get yourself back on your feet, so there shouldn't be a problem. All I want is the best for our Cameron."

I let out a small laugh and shook my head as I said, "Funny how a few quid in your pocket can make you change your mind, isn't it? I know fine well where your priorities lie, and they're not with Cameron."

Clive nudged past me as he came into the living room, and sat on the floor by Sandra, and bravely added, "She said it was okay Mark, now lay off."

My attention turned to Clive, and I warned him, "Listen up meat head. This has got fuck all to do with you. It's between me, Sandra and *my* son. So I suggest that you button that fat mouth of yours, before I lay you out, again."

As Clive shrank, I returned my attention to Sandra and continued, "Right, I'll pop over every Friday afternoon, starting from next week, to give you Cameron's money."

Before with of them were given the chance to reply, I turned and walked out. I didn't want to stay in that house any longer than I had to, especially while my son was sleeping.

As I drove off, I noticed Clive standing at the window, staring at me. I gave him a big false smile and a girlish wave. I think I need to find out a little more about this twat. It wouldn't be difficult to find him; I'd only have to search around the nearby gymnasiums and solariums.

Chapter 10

After our eventful evening at Liberties, Lurch, Jez, Nick and I decided it would be a better idea to have a quiet night at the club. We also decided that we would be pushing our luck by having another nigh in at my home, as I don't think mum would be too enthusiastic about it.

Jez and I arrived first, and to save any arguments I went to the bar and bought four beers. As I was returning to the table, Nick and Lurch came in. Perfect timing. It made a nice change being able to talk normally, without having to shout over loud thumping music, just to be able to hear each other. It was also quite nice not having to queue up at the bar for ages then have some skinny little pissed up dickhead push into the front without waiting their turn. I also forced the lads into making a temporary pact for the night- no taking the piss out of Lurch.

After many bottles of beer, a few games of pool and Nick winning fifty quid at the bingo, we decided to call it a night. I had a lesson booked for in the morning so I didn't want to risk turning up for work stinking of alcohol.

Nick and Lurch's taxi arrived, So Jez and I made our way on foot, as it wasn't that far away for us to walk.

Jez didn't have much to say during the journey home, and I could sense there was something bothering him.

"You haven't said much tonight mate. You okay?" I asked him.

"To be honest mate," Jez replied, "I'm getting myself a bit chewed up a bit over you. Think you've got a few issues that need sorting before you explode."

"There's nothing wrong mate," I assured him, ""Aye I've got a few issues going on in my head, but it's nothing to get your knob in a know over. I just can't get a grip of the way other people are. Half the people around here don't even know how to spell the word respect, never mind know what it means."

"I know Mark," Jez continued, "But you always take it to the extreme. The slightest thing makes you blow your top. One of these days, you're gonna end up inside or in a bloody coffin. You might be able to look after yourself mate, but one day you might not be so lucky."

"Nah," I contested, "I'll be okay, and I'm slowly getting there. My work's keeping me focused."

There were a few more seconds of silence before Jez stopped in his tracks and asked, "Can I ask you a bit of a personal question, mate?"

Aye, fire away mate, I don't mind." I replied with a smile.

Jez took a deep breathe and paused before continuing, "What do you think of the army? And, do you miss it?"

"Oh fuck, Jez. I miss it loads mate." I replied, "But at the same time, I fucking despise it. I feel robbed. To the hierarchy I was nothing but a fucking number. It was one fucking rule for the soldiers and a different set of rules for the officers. You know, fuck all happened to those two twats who I caught humping Sandra!"

"Yes, I know mate," Jez acknowledged, "They should've had their fucking balls cut off."

"Nah," I laughed, "they didn't have one bollock between them. Neither of them had a fucking spine either."

After a short pause, I decided it was time to slightly change the subject by mentioning Clive.

"You know this arsehole that Sandra's seeing?" I asked.

"Oh the spray tanned fuck wit." Jez acknowledged with a smirk.

"Well do you know anything about him? I want to find out more about him. At the end of the day, there's a fucking stranger living with my son." I asked.

"Don't think that would be difficult mate," Jez said, "Castletown's quite a small place, so it would be a good place to start."

"Think I need to do some stalking first," I said as my mind started working, "I need to find out where he hangs out, where he drinks, who his mates are."

"Well," Jez said, "I don't mind giving you a hand Mark, just as long as it doesn't go too far. I'm not into any of that mercenary shite."

Since beginning my maintenance arrangements with Sandra, I made a point of having no lessons booked on a Friday afternoon. I made my usual trip to Castletown to give Sandra the money, but on this occasion I brought Jez with me in his car. We parked at the bottom of the street, out of sight of the house, and I walked up to the door leaving Jez in the car.

Clive answered the door as usual, and I noticed the puzzled look on his face, as he poked his head out and looked left and right for my van.

"It's in the garage for its MOT, sweetheart." I said, reading his mind, "Now are you going to let me in, or am I going to stand here looking as fucking dumb as you?"

He shuffled his huge carcass to one side, allowing me to squeeze past him, and I walked into the living room to find Sandra rooted to her usual spot on the sofa watching the usual crap on the television. I took the money out of my jacket pocket and gave it to her. No words were exchanged until I asked where Cameron was.

"He's at my mam's." she answered whilst counting the money, "I'm just having a bit of a break."

"So what's wrong with asking me to have him?" I asked, "After all, I am his fucking dad!"

"No, it was a last minute thing," she lied, "She was down here earlier, and just asked if she could take him out for the day."

I reached into my pocket and pulled out one of my

business cards and gave it to Sandra saying, "Look, next time you fancy a break, give me a ring and I'll come and get him. You not think it's about time he spent some quality time with his dad?"

"I'll see," she replied as she placed my card on the coffee table in front of her.

As Clive walked into the room, I noticed that he had obviously mistakenly taken some bravery pills instead of his horse steroids, because he squared up to me with his chest puffed out.

He looked me up and down, then stared into my eyes and said, "Look, gobshite. I'm getting a bit fucking sick of you coming into *my* house and calling the shots."

I grabbed him by his neck and pushed him back against the wall and spat in his face and said, "Your house? Maybe, but my son lives here, and as far as my son's concerned you can go take your face for a shit. And I think I've got every right to be ever so fucking irate now and again. So I suggest you sit your pretty arse down, before I knock you down. And remember, if I want your opinion, I'll fucking give you it."

I held onto his neck for a few more seconds, then let go just before he was reaching the point of passing out through lack of oxygen. He dropped to the floor in a crumpled heap clutching his throat, gasping. And I turned my attention back to Sandra.

"Like I said," I continued, "You've got my number now, so just let me know when I can have Cameron. And do me a favour; sort your lover boy out with his mouth, because he's really starting to boil my piss. I'll see myself out. See you next week."

I walked out of the house, and slammed the door behind me, and then I sprinted down the street to Jez and the car before the bronzed Adonis had recovered and thought about having another pop. When I got into the car I began to laugh, and Jez was looking at me puzzled.

"What the bloody hell are you laughing at? What you done?" he asked.

"That fuckwit pushes his luck every time I go there. He

just doesn't fucking learn, because every time I just send him off with his tail between his legs." I replied.

"You smacked him again?" Jez asked laughing with me.

"No, I just pinned him up against the wall by his throat when he squared up to me." I replied, "God I'd love to just kick the shit out of him."

"His time will come, mate." Jez added, "One day he will fall flat on his arse."

"Right," I said, more seriously, "well for now I want us to sit here and wait to see of Clivey boy comes out. And if he does, we'll see where he leads us."

Jez reached over onto his back seats and grabbed two newspapers, and handed me one saying, "Well, if we're going to be here for a while, we might as well have something to do."

Just as I was becoming enthralled in a gripping story in my copy of the Daily Sport, I briefly looked up and saw Clive coming out of the house. He was wearing a black suit and black overcoat, and actually looked quite smart. He walked to the top of the street and turned left towards the shops, so Jez slowly drove up the street and stopped at the corner so we could see him without him actually being able to spot us. Clive was waiting at the bus stop, but it wasn't long before a bus arrived and he got onto it.

We followed the bus, ensuring we remained far away enough as not to cause any suspicion. The bus had driven into a nearby estate known as Hylton Castle, and Clive got off when it reached the small shopping area. We pulled into the parking area in front of the shops, and watched Clive walk straight past us where he entered a door which appeared to lead up to a small office upstairs. There was a small brass plaque screwed to the heavy looking door, but I couldn't quite make out the engraving on it. I paused for a minute or two, then got out of the car and quickly walked over to the door. My heart missed a beat when I read the plaque. Across the top in bold capital letters was the company name -"Epic Security Company". In a smaller font underneath the title was Eric Barnes' name. My skin crawled.

I sprinted back to the car, and as soon as I sat back in my seat, I told Jez to drive.

"What do you know about Eric Barnes, Jez?" I asked.

"Oh, he's a dodgy fucker," Jez replied, "In his time he was a right bastard apparently. He's getting on a bit now, so he gets other nutters to do the dirty work for him. Done time for attempted murder, GBH, arson, you name it. He owns most of the bouncers that work the town pubs."

"I take it that's what Epic Security's all about then. Bouncers." I said, "Well he's apparently sending a couple of his men around to see me to have a chat about me using his services."

"Aye," Jez replied, "but I've heard that he used his bouncers to force money out of shops and small businesses in the area. And if they don't pay, things happen. Like a protection racquet I suppose."

"Ah, fucking brilliant!" I exclaimed with sarcasm. "Looks like I'm going to have a bunch of bully boys chasing after me for money then. Best keep myself on my toes from now on then."

"Looks like Sandra's knob head of a boyfriend's working for him too, by the looks of it, mate." Jez continued, "So I think you'd better be careful what you're saying to him from now on mate."

"Nah," I said, "fuck him. He's soft as shite and thick as a fucking submarine door."

"Well just be careful Mark," Jez warned me, "As long as you realise that things could get quite messy if you get involved with them lot."

I looked at Jez and smiled, "They best not fuck with me then."

Jez shook his head in disbelief with my last comment and said, "Look Mark, you won't be dealing with a bunch of pissed up yobs here. They fuck people over for a living. Eric and his lads are a bunch of nasty bastards, and I don't think you should be messing with them. We're talking knives and fucking guns here mate! Eric's even got himself in with a few of the police apparently, making him almost untouchable. He's that fucking big, man! So please just do me one favour and try and keep them sweet, and be careful with that frigging idiot Clive. He might be a soft shite, but if he's got Eric's backing, you're fucked."

"I do see where you're coming from Jez," I replied, "But at the end of the day, I'm not going to sit back and let some meat head bully come and wreck my life or my business. Also, if that Clive is as dodgy as his boss, I'm not happy with my son being around him. I've seen the way he talks to him, and I fucking dread to think what he's like when I'm not around. No one hurts my boy, Jez. No fucker!"

"Fair enough mate," Jez said, "But id Eric or his lads put you in hospital, or worse, you won't be around to be able to do anything for your Cameron. I'm not saying to just take the shit; I just want you to be careful."

"Well let's just see what happens first, eh?" I said, "Like I said, I might be getting a visit from a couple of his lads within the next couple of days soon, so I'll just keep my eyes peeled for now, and play it by ear."

Jez dropped me off at home, and as I opened the front door, I heard my mother shout from the kitchen.

"Is that you, son? I'm in the kitchen; you must've heard me putting the kettle on."

"Aye, go on then," I replied, "Milk and two sugars please."

I walked into the living room and slouched on the sofa, wondering what I could do with myself. It was Friday after all, and I didn't have any lessons booked for tomorrow. Jez was working a late shift tonight, so a few quiet pints with him was out of the question. I switched the television on and checked the listings to see if anything decent was on. Nothing.

Mum came into the room carrying two cups of coffee and she walked straight through into the dining area and placed them on the table. One of her many house rules was that no one was allowed food or drink in the sitting room on the sofa. I walked over to the table and sat opposite her and took a few sips from my coffee. My mother watched me as I drank and when I placed my cup back on the table she asked if I was okay.

"Aye, I'm fine, mam." I replied.

Sorry son," she said, "I'm not buying that. I know you, and I know something's bothering you. Now what's up?"

I sat back in the chair and sighed, not really wanting to worry her with what was going on, and with what could happen. There was no way of keeping it from her; she could read me like a book. And she'd kill me if she heard it from someone else.

"I've just found out that Sandra's fella is working for a dodgy firm called Epic Security. I've also had a phone call from the firm's boss...."

Before I could finish, my mother interrupted, "Oh please don't say you're getting involved with that Barnes bloke. He's bad news, and he's bloody dangerous."

"No, no," I tried to assure her, "He rang me up asking if I wanted protection for my business, but I politely declined. I've just got a feeling that he's got a problem with rejection, and that I haven't heard the last of him."

"Well if you get any trouble from him or any of his workers, make sure you ring the police, Mark. I'm not paying you any more visits to that damned hospital. And I don't want you thinking you can take on the world by yourself. No heroics, okay?" she demanded.

I could see my mother's eyes welling up with tears so I reached over the table and held her hands. I looked into her eyes and smiled.

"Look, mam." I said, "I don't go around looking for trouble you know. I'll be okay, now stop your flapping."

There was a knock at the door which made us both jump. I signalled for my mum to stay where she was and I went to answer it. It was Lurch and Nick, and they were both dressed for a night out.

"Get your glad rags on Mark," Lurch ordered, "We're off out on the tiles, and you're coming with us."

"Where you got in mind, like?" I asked them both.

"Thought you might fancy coming into town." Lurch replied.

"OH, I don't know if I can be fucked on with the town, lads." I replied, shrugging my shoulders.

"AH, ha'way man, Mark." Nick pleaded, "There'll be no bother, and if anything, we could all do with a decent night out."

My mother popped her head into the hallway and interrupted, "Come on in boys. There's a couple of beers in the fridge you can help yourselves to while Mark nips upstairs to get ready."

I stepped to one side and ushered Nick and Lurch in.

"I guess this means I'm coming out with you both then." I said as I ran upstairs.

The taxi dropped us off in the town centre, and as soon as I stepped out of the car, I could hear the music pounding out of the surrounding pubs and clubs. Crowds of people were flocking from bar to bar, and others were crowded outside pub entrances, smoking and drinking. There were small gaggles of women scattered all over, and I watched them as they hung onto each other in drunken stupors, laughing and swearing.

We walked into a busy bar, and the moment I opened the door to enter, I could feel the vibrations from the music shaking up through my feet and rattling my knee caps. We fought our way through the crowds towards the bar, and I shouted for three beers. There was no way I was wanting to stand here, where the music was almost rupturing my ear drums, so I signalled for us to go out to the beer garden where it wouldn't be as deafening.

As soon as we finished our beers, we moved onto another bar, then another, the another. There wasn't much conversation between us, mainly due to the fact that the music in every bar was way too loud. The only opportunity we had to speak properly was when we were outside, and even then we still had to shout.

The three of us went into a small, but still very busy, bar, and the DJ was playing some sort of base-heavy dance music. The room was packed with young people, and the dance floor was filled with drunken idiots jumping around to the music. We made our way to the bar and waited our turn to be served. Just as a space cleared and I was about to step forwards towards the bar, a young man came from behind and nudged past me to the space in front and ordered some drinks.

I tapped him on the shoulder, and when he turned around to face me I asked, "Erm, excuse me mate, but do you not do queuing up and waiting your turn?"

He looked me up and down, then turned back to the bar, ignoring my question.

"Oi!" I shouted, "I asked you a question. Do you not believe in waiting your turn?"

The lad looked over his shoulder and muttered, "Fuck off, loser. You snooze, you lose."

Lurch came by my side and shook his head, telling me to just leave it. So I waited until the lad had been served. The second he picked up his drinks and turned, I stepped forward and barged forward, making him drop his drinks on the floor.

"What the fuck you playing at, you daft bastard?" the lad moaned.

"Oh, sorry," I apologised sarcastically, "I was just trying to get at the bar, mate. Didn't see you there."

"Well you best be getting me some fucking drinks in then while you're there." He said, threateningly.

I stood in front of him with my arms crossed over my

chest, defiantly, and said, "Well if you had waited your turn, like any normal polite person, then maybe it wouldn't have happened. And maybe if you had any manners, you would've said 'excuse me', and I would've moved out your way. Now how's about you fuck off back to the end of the queue, and reorder your drinks, and this time, try and not be so fucking ignorant."

The young lad puffed out his chest and squared up to me and said, "Erm, no. How's about you fuck off. After you've bought me the drinks you made me spill."

As we squared up to each other, and just as things were about to get interesting, I felt a hand firmly grip my shoulder and I was pulled backwards. Lurch dragged me away from the bar and suggested we all leave. I tried contesting, but neither Lurch or Nick were in the mood for getting involved in any hassle, so I eventually gave up and left.

"What the fuck you playing at, man?" Nick asked.

"Did you not see that little twat?" I replied, "He just barged past me, not giving a shit!"

Lurch then suggested, "You seriously need to chill out mate. We've come out for a good night out, not a fight."

"Well if people weren't so fucking ignorant, I wouldn't get do worked up and stroppy." I added.

"Tell you what," Lurch went on, "Don't know about you two, but I'm feeling a bit peckish now. So how about we just grab a kebab and head home. Think we'll call it a night eh?"

Nick and I both nodded in agreement, so we headed for the take away shop before heading home in a taxi.

Chapter 11

I had just finished another Sunday "Early Birds" session, and as nothing else was booked in, I gave Lucy the rest of the day off. Once she had closed the computer down, she picked up her handbag and left. I then made myself a coffee and sat at the desk with my feet up.

Just as I was beginning to relax, I heard the front door swing open and heavy footsteps heading down the corridor. It certainly didn't sound like Lucy coming back. As I took my feet off the desk and straightened myself up, two men walked into the office. They were both dressed in dark suits and highly polished shoes. The man on the left was at least six feet tall, and almost the same in width, with a shaven head and some sort of tribal tattoo on the side of his face. His associate was short but stocky, with long dark greased back hair, and the false tan could not quite hide the scar beneath his left eye.

I stood up out of my chair and welcomed them.

"Alright lads? I'm Mark, and I take it you're from Epic Security. Please, take a seat."

"Thank you." Grunted big baldy bloke as they both undid their jackets and sat on the sofa in the corner of the office.

I, on the other hand, decided to remain on my feet, in case I needed to move quickly. So I walked over to the small table and offered to make them a coffee. Neither of them wanted one, but I made a fresh one for myself.

I stood in front of my desk, and leaned back against it, facing the pair. After taking a quick sip from my coffee, I placed the cup on my desk behind me, and started the inevitable.

"Well then, gentlemen. What can I do you for?" I asked whilst forcing a smile.

"As you already know, Mr Harrison," big baldy bloke answered, "Mr Barnes has offered our services to you, and I've been made aware that you have refused his offer. Many of the businesses around here have taken us on, and take full advantage of our business. I would hate to have to go back to Mr Barnes and informed him of your lack of co operation, as he would be deeply offended."

I folded my arms across my chest, and continued to question, "So what exactly are you offering me? What sort of protection do you provide?"

The short stocky guy moved forward to the edge of his seat to give his input, "We will basically be on permanent twenty four hour stand by for you. If you ever have any problems, you give us a ring and we come and sort it. Simple as that."

"Well, I'm not being funny, lads, but I'm big and daft enough to look after myself. And unfortunately, I don't see the point of paying someone to do a job that I can do myself. Anyway, what happens from here, what with me refusing your services and all that?"

Big baldy bloke shook his head and sighed, "When Mr Barnes offers his services, it's always advisable to take him up on his offer. I'm sure you will understand when I say that upsetting him is not a wise move."

I walked around to the other side of my desk, giving me space between me and the two heavies, and said, "Well, you can tell Mr Barnes that, with the up most respect, I don't need or want your so called services. I've managed on my own so far, and I'm happy with the way things are. So thanks, but no thanks."

"Well," the huge guy spoke as he stood back up, "I really do hope you realise what you have just signed yourself up for by turning us down. Good luck with your business, you're going to need it, sunshine."

The short stocky man stood up to join his comrade, and the both buttoned up their jackets in unison, like a well rehearsed act.

As they walked out of the office, the short man paused briefly and turned to me saying, "See you around Mark. Oh, and say hello to your mam, Marge, for me."

I stood at my desk and waited for the door to slam shut then dropped into my chair. Giving out a huge sigh.

"Bollocks," I thought to myself, "What the fuck's going to happen now? They must know fucking everything about me. Oh well, looks like they've got a fight on their hands, because no matter how bad they are, no one fucks with my family. I'll kill the bastards!"

I reached down into the bottom desk drawer and pulled out the miniature bottle of brandy that I keep for personal medicinal purposes. I unscrewed the cap and poured the liquid into my mouth. My throat burned as the brandy flowed down into my stomach and I could feel my body tingle as I relaxed. I sat back and put my feet up on the desk, and took another large gulp from the bottle.

The place was so quiet my ears began to ring and my head buzzed. I closed my eyes, and the usual twisted thought began entering my mind again. The two men who tried robbing me at the bank were stood there next to Clive, Sandra and the two meat heads who had just left. They were all laughing at me, and as I attempted to shake away their images, their laughing became more and more hysterical. My head was now pounding, and my heart was racing. My palms were cold and clammy, and sweat dripped from my brow. I could feel my body slowly tense as it filled with rage, and the images refused to go away. I walked out of the office into the exercise room towards the boxing area, and put on a pair of training gloves. I stood in front of one of the boxing bags and began jabbing with my left fist. The speed and ferocity of my jobs gradually increased, and I added my right fist to alternate my punches. My breathing became heavier, and sweat dripped from my face. I punched harder and faster until the bag was swinging all over. I hammered a right hook into the bag with all of my might, and the sheer force sent the bag flying off its hook, and landed with a thud on the floor. I threw the gloves from my hands and headed back into the office. I was exhausted, but felt elated. I grabbed my keys, locked up the unit and sat in the van. As soon as I started the engine, I turned up the stereo to full volume with the hope of drowning out the sounds already in my head.

The drive home was a total blur, as if I was on auto pilot. I sat in the van for a few moments outside the house, before switching it off and getting out. I needed something to do, and quick. No way was I allowing any harm to come to my family, so I needed to strike first before they had the chance.

I opened the front door to the house and shouted to check if mum was in. She must've gone out to bingo with Aunt Linda. I made myself a coffee and sat at the dining table, wondering what to do next. My head was buzzing with thoughts, trying to think logically about what to do. These idiots know my mother's name, so do they know where I live? Is Cameron going to be safe? What do I say to my mother? Will she think it's all my fault?

I drained the last few drops of coffee out of my cup, and then went upstairs to have a shower and get changed. Once I was dressed, I grabbed my keys and went back out to the van. My mother was out, so there's nothing I can do as far as she's concerned. And I don't think she'd appreciate it if I went storming into the bingo hall. I will wait until she gets home. I decided that, for now, my priority was Cameron, so I drove down to Castletown to speak to Sandra.

I parked the van directly outside her house, and before I got out, I reached into the glove compartment and pulled out my telescopic baton, and slipped it up my left sleeve. This was kept in my van for emergencies, since the incident at the bank. I knocked on the door, and Sandra quickly answered.

"What do you want?" she asked unenthusiastically.

"I've just come for a quick chat, Sandra, I won't keep you

long." I replied.

Sandra stepped to one side, allowing me into her house and said, "Well if you've come to give Clive another smacking you've shit out, because he's out."

Ignoring her comment, I walked through to the living room and sat on the sofa. As usual, the television was blaring out the usual shit, so I picked up the remote control and turned the television off.

"Fucking hell, Mark!" Sandra cursed as she walked in to the room, "Make yourself at home, why don't you?"

"Look," I insisted, "No fucking about, I've come to have a quick word with you. And I want some answers."

Sandra sat down on the floor in front of the gas fire and looked up at me, "So what do you want then?"

"Where's Cameron, by the way?" I asked, ignoring her question for now.

"He's in bed," she answered, "Is that all you've come for?"

"Oh, no!" I said, "I've come about Clivey boy."

Sandra shifted about on the floor, looking quite uncomfortable now, and said nothing.

I leaned forward, resting my elbows on my knees, and looked her straight into her eyes.

"At the moment, I don't know much about Clive. And what I'm starting to find out, I don't like. And I'm hoping that my son's not going to get caught up in something bad."

"Well, I don't know what you've found out or been told," she said insolently, "But Clive's a good bloke, and he looks after us both."

"So what does he do? Does he work?" I pressed.

"Aye," she answered nervously, "He's a security guard."

"And where does he work? Who for?" I continued to interrogate.

Sandra appeared even more irate from my constant

questioning, and stood up and folded her arms across her chest.

"What's your problem, Mark? You jealous?" she asked.

I remained seated as I mocked her, "Ha! I'm not jealous at all sweetheart. He's fucking welcome to you. I'm just concerned about who's living with my son. You do know that Clive works for Eric Barnes, don't you?"

Sandra immediately jumped to Clive's defence, "That doesn't make him a dodgy twat though Mark. He works hard, and brings in good money for us. Like I said, he looks after us, and for your information, he's actually quite good with Cameron."

I stood up and took a step towards Sandra, "I know fine well what Barnes's blokes are like. I'm having a few dealings with them myself, and it looks like things could get a bit nasty. So I will warn you now and please pass this onto lover boy when he gets back in - If anyone harms my boy they will have me to answer to. I don't care who they are, or how fucking hard they think they are, no one hurts my bairn. I couldn't give a shit what you get up to, you can rot in hell for all I care. But if anyone so much as breathes on Cameron the wrong way, I'll fucking kill them. Understand?"

Sandra could tell by the glint in my eyes that I wasn't fooling around, and she now looked afraid. But she shook her head and said, "You don't scare me Mark. You're just a fucking nutter. If anything happens to anyone, it'll be down to you, because you're out of control and you look for trouble."

I laughed in her face and continued my verbal onslaught, "You haven't got a fucking clue what's going on with me, and you never will. I'm not looking for trouble, but if anyone hurts my boy, I will certainly be bringing trouble to your door. And I will be walking away from here with my son. Trust me, you won't be able to stop me."

Sandra was about to open her foul mouth again, but I put my hand in the air, stopping her in her tracks, "Ah, conversation over. I've said what I wanted to say, and I'm not interested in listening to your shite. What you say to Clive is up to you, but just bare in mind what I've just told you."

I walked to the living room door and tuned to Sandra, saying, "Sit down, sweetheart. I'll see myself out."

My mother came back from the bingo as I was sat on the sofa watching the television. As soon as I heard her come through the front door, I shot up out of my seat and dashed into the kitchen to put the kettle on. She followed me into the kitchen, and I noticed she was grinning from ear to ear.

"Come on then," I said, "How much did you win tonight?"

"Me and your Aunty Linda won eight grand between us on the National!" She screamed as she threw her arms around me.

"Well done," I congratulated her, "Just remember how much you love me though."

"Oh I've already got it spend, love," she said excitedly, "Me and Aunty Linda are going away for a week in Tenerife, then when I get back I'm going to give this place a lick of paint. I haven't decorated in here for a few years now."

"Well, you enjoy it mam," I said as I hugged her, "You deserve it. And don't worry, I won't make too much mess while you're away."

"You'd better bloody not, lad." she said as she waved a finger in my face and still smiling.

I took our coffees through to the dining room and we both sat in our usual places. Because of the good mood she was in, I decided not to mention anything yet about what's been going on. I didn't want to ruin her moment.

The noise of broken glass downstairs made me jump out of bed, and as I ran out of my room to go and investigate, my mother was walking out of her room whilst putting on her dressing gown. Luckily, I was wearing my shorts. I told her to stay in her room, and I ran downstairs to check.

The front door was still fully in tact, so I went into the living room. A house brick was lay in the middle of the floor, and broken glass was scattered all over the room. The brick had obviously been thrown through the front window. I ran outside in the hope of catching someone, but the street was dead. A few lights had flickered on in some of the houses opposite us, but there was no one actually in the street. I ran back into the house, and grabbed a brush from under the stairs, and began cleaning up the mess.

"This got anything to do with the Barnes's boys, by any chance?" my mother asked as she walked into the living room.

I stopped sweeping, looked up at her and said, "More than likely, mam. I had a visit from two of them the other day at work, and I refused to pay into their protection racquet. I didn't realise they would do something like this though."

Mum went into the hallway, and I heard her pick up the telephone. I threw the brush down and ran out to her, grabbing the phone out of her hand.

"Don't even think of ringing the coppers, mam," I warned her, "That would only make matters worse, wouldn't it? And at the end of the day, how can we prove it was them that did this?"

"Well it looks like this could get messy son, and I don't like it. I'm not having them thugs coming and wrecking my bloody home. So I suggest you get this sorted, and now!" Mum demanded, "Whatever it takes, you end this trouble, before it really gets out of hand. You understand?"

"Leave it with me mam," I replied, "I'll sort it all out, I promise."

As she got to the bottom of the stairs, she turned to me and said, "You'd better, because I'm still going on my bloody holiday with Linda, and those bastards aren't spoiling it for me."

Chapter 12

I arrived early at work to cancel any bookings that had been made, and I contacted Lucy to say she could have the day off. Although I was in work, I kept the window shutters down, and the doors locked to avoid any unwanted attention.

I contacted Jez, Nick and Lurch, asking them to come to the unit and that it was a matter of urgency. Within twenty minutes there was a knock at the door, and I opened it to let the three of them in. Once they were in, I locked the door again.

While they were making themselves comfortable, I made four cups of coffee. Instead of using milk, I added a splash of cream liqueur to each cup and handed them out.

"Oh we are getting spoiled," Nick said, "What you after?"

I laughed and replied, "Now what makes you think I'm after something?"

Jez wasn't laughing when he piped up and said, "Well I've got a feeling what this is all about."

I walked around to my desk and sat in my chair. Took a quick sip from my coffee then placed it on my desk before filling them all in on what's been happening.

"Right," I said, "Eric Barnes and his boys paid me a visit the other day and I basically told them to shove their protection up their arses. Then, at daft o'clock this morning, a fucking brick was put through my living room window. Now it doesn't take the brains of an arch bishop to work out that it was one of them twats who did it. They obviously know where I work and live, but they also know my mother's name, and I've got a feeling that things are going to get fucking nasty with them. I've got you all here now, because I want to know if any of you are willing to help me put a stop to this before it goes too far. I want to get it nipped in the bed before someone gets hurt."

"Is paying the protection money not an option, Mark?" Lurch asked.

"No chance, mate," I replied, "Those fuckers are not getting any of my hard earned cash just to stop them from getting at me. No one threatens me, Lurch. You should know that by now. And I'll be wasting my time getting the coppers involved, so I need to get this sorted, now."

"So what are you suggesting we do, mate?" Jez asked.

"I'm not entirely sure yet, mate," I replied, "But my mam's going away on holiday, and I need to get it sorted by the time she gets back. I don't care what it takes, I want it sorting so they leave my family alone."

Jez smiled, pointed at Lurch and Nick and said, "Well I don't know about Dumb and Dumber here, but you can count me in Mark.

Lurch and Nick looked at each other, and then looked at me and both said, "Aye, count us in as well."

"Champion!" I said, "Well I'll get my thinking cap on, and when I'm sorted with a plan of action, I'll give you all a shout."

The lads all nodded in agreement, so I stood up and waved my cup at them, "Right, who's for a cheeky little top up?"

Just as I was making my way over to the table, there was a loud knocking at the front door. All four of us looked at each other, wondering who it might be. I walked out of the office and along the corridor, with the lads close behind me. I turned the key in the door to unlock it and Sandra came barging through pushing Cameron in his pram. Cameron was crying. I quickly looked out the door, an could see the car parked randomly in front of the unit, with the engine still running.

I followed Sandra as she marched down the corridor towards my office, and I asked the boys to wait out in the corridor for a while.

What's up Sandra? Why's Cameron crying?" I asked.

"I'm fucked if I know!" she replied aggressively, "He hasn't stopped crying since yesterday, and I've been up all fucking night with him!"

"I take it you had a good night last night though. I can still smell the fucking beer on you!" I pointed out.

"That's got fuck all to do with you, Mark!" she yelled, "I just had a few drinks to keep me going while I was up all night."

"Jesus Christ, woman!" I screamed, "You're probably still pissed now, and you're fucking driving about with my son in the car with you. Remind me, who's the fucking nutter? Me or you?"

"Oh fuck off Mark," she cursed, "Whatever I do has got nothing to do with you any more"

"When it involves my son, I would say it's got quite a fucking lot to do with me, Sandra." I replied.

Sandra continued to scream at me, and pushed the pram into my legs, "Well if you think you can do a better fucking job than me, crack on. Let's see how much of a father you really are. I'm off!"

Sandra stormed out of the office, and as I followed her I asked Jez to keep an eye on Cameron. The front door almost came off its hinges when Sandra swung it open, and she stormed over to the car, almost fell into it and slammed the door behind her.

I stood at the unit door and watched as she pulled away, noticing that the car was swaying all over the road. She was definitely still drunk. Just as I was heading back into the unit, my head spun back round at the sound of a screech and a loud bang. Sandra had driven to the end of the road, but must have been going way too fast to be able to stop at the junction, and ploughed the car head on into the wall on the other side of the road.

Lurch and Nick came running out, followed by Jez pushing Cameron in his pram. I asked Jez to stay with Cameron, who was still crying, and then grabbed Lurch as I sprinted towards the battered car. The front end of the car was totally smashed in, with steam spewing out of what was left of the front grille, and broken glass scattered the road. Sandra was hanging out of the windscreen lying face down over the crumpled bonnet. Her face was splattered in blood and her eyes were wide open, but motionless. She wasn't moving or making a sound. As I neared her, I noticed a huge gash in her head, and blood was oozing out the wound. I came to the conclusion that not only was she drunk, but she was also driving without wearing her seatbelt.

While I was attempting to revive her, Lurch rang for an ambulance on his mobile phone. She was losing blood at a rapid rate, and I could barely feel a pulse. I ripped off my shirt and wrapped it around her head in the hope it would stem the bleeding enough until the paramedics arrived, but within seconds my shirt was sodden with blood.

By the time the ambulance arrived, there was no hope for Sandra. She was pronounced dead at the scene. Her body was taken away for further investigation into the cause of death, and the police arrived to investigate the scene of the accident. After I had given a statement, the police then arranged for the damaged car to be towed away and checked over.

My body felt numb, and I couldn't understand why I felt no emotion. I should be crying my eyes out by now, but I just sat there in my office, staring into nothingness. I was brought back into reality when the boys walked in, and I saw Jez pushing Cameron. My son was fast asleep, and looked so peaceful.

I looked at Jez then down at Cameron, and said, "My boy could've been in that car there. The stupid bitch could've killed my lad!"

"Well she hasn't mate," he replied, "He's here, safe and sound."

Lurch put the kettle on and made us all a coffee. While Cameron was sleeping, we all sat in the office, not a word was uttered. All I could do was stare at Cameron, thinking how close he was to being in that car with Sandra when it crashed.

"Right!" I finally broke the silence, "This doesn't change what we were talking about earlier. We've still got things to sort out. But now I have more reason to get this sorted sooner rather than later now, I've got Cameron to look after."

"Well, we're definitely behind with this mate. Anything you want, just let us know, okay?" Jez said.

"Thanks lads," I replied, "Well I think I'd better get this little one home to see his Nana Fucking hell, how am I going to explain this one without her thinking I done Sandra over."

"Aye," Nick said, "She's in for one hell of a fucking surprise mate."

As I didn't have a child safety seat for Cameron, I walked home with him while he continued to sleep in his pram. When I got there, mum was out, so I wheeled Cameron into the living room and let him sleep while I re arranged the spare room to make space for his things. Once my mother was home, I would have to pop out and but him a new bed and some essentials. I could quite easily collect his belongings from Castletown later.

After an hour or so had passed, I heard the front door open and I heard my mother shout for me up the stairs. I noticed the extremely puzzled look on here face as I walked down.

"Erm, I take it that Sandra's okay with you having Cameron?" she asked.

I walked straight past her into the living room and sat on the sofa. When my mum had followed me in, I said, "I think you'd better sit down, mam. Something's happened."

My mother was totally dumbfounded over what had happened, but it wasn't long before she warmed to the thought of having Cameron with us on a permanent basis.

"There's obviously going to be an investigation into how and why it happened, mam." I continued to tell her, "But there won't be any problems with Cameron being here with us. At the end of the day, I'm his dad."

Mum raised her eyebrows and said, "Well if anyone tried getting in between you and Cameron, they've got to get through me first. Me and you will look after our boy, and we will bring him up right."

"Thanks mam," I said, "I knew I could rely on you. But I need to ask you a favour."

"Come on then," she said with her eyebrows still raised, "What you after?"

"You know this carry on I'm having with Eric Barnes and his yobbos?" I asked, "Well, while you're away, I'm planning on getting it all sorted. But I'm not really going to be able to get much done while Cameron's here now."

"I've got a feeling where this is heading." mum interrupted with a smirk.

"If I give you the money, would you mind taking our Cameron on holiday with you and Aunty Linda? I really don't want Cameron being in the firing line, if anything gets out of hand, that's all."

"Hey, you don't have to ask twice, son." mum beamed from ear to ear, "I would love to take him with me, it'd be nice to spend some quality time with him and get to know him actually. But I will have to check with your Aunty Linda, mind."

I went over to where my mother was sitting and gave her a big hug, "Thank you mam. You're on angel."

My mum returned the hug and said, "Look Mark, doesn't matter how old you are, you're my boy. And I am so bloody proud of you and that little boy of yours over there. I will do absolutely anything for my family, and don't you ever forget that. I'm hoping that things don't get too nasty, but I'm sure that you'll get this mess sorted. In time, we will be sorted."

"Right," I said, "Well I'd better get started with sorting things out right now. I'm going to pop out and get some things for Cameron. I've shifted a few things round in the spare room so I can at least get a bed in there. I might even pop down to Castletown later, and grab some of his things from there."

Mum pointed over to the other side of the room and said, "Pass my handbag from over there and I'll give you some money towards everything."

"No, don't worry about it, mam." I protested, "I'll be okay, I've got enough dosh."

"Don't be so bloody soft, lad." she said as she went over for her handbag herself.

She took her purse out the handbag, and handed me a great wad of notes. There must have been at least four hundred pounds.

"Come on mam, you don't have to give me all that." I pleaded with her.

"Take it!" mum insisted, "We're in this together, and looking after a child isn't cheap. So take the money, there's plenty more where that came from." You're going to need all the help you can get, and that's what I'm here for."

Including the money I got from my mother, I returned from the retail park well over a thousand pounds lighter. My mother was bloody right. I knew that Cameron would probably have plenty of things back at his old home in Castletown, but the more I thought about going there, the less appealing the idea sounded. I had no need to go back there any more

I kitted out his bedroom with a new bed and wardrobe, and decorated the room with toys and pictures. At the end of his bed was a large wicker basket filled with toys. My mother had found some old framed pictures of teddy bears, which used to belong to me many moons ago. She dusted them down and hung them on the walls in his room. She also placed at the end of his bed a tatty old teddy bear dressed in combat uniform and red beret. My father had bought it for my mother years ago, and, until now, it had been gathering dust in the attic.

While I was out shopping, my mother had contacted Aunt Linda, so she came round to the house to see us all. I was sat on the living room floor entertaining Cameron when she arrived, and she burst into tears of joy the instant she walked into the room. I stood up as she came in and she gave me a huge bear hug.

"I know the circumstances could've been a lot better son," she said in between sobs, "But I'm over the moon that he's here with you, where he belongs. I know you will be good for him. And if you need anything, just let me know. Absolutely anything."

I gave Aunt Linda a kiss on the cheek and thanked her. We looked down at Cameron as he climbed up onto his feet and toddled towards me with his arms outstretched towards me. This caused my mother and Aunt Linda to burst into more floods of tears again, especially as I crouched down to pick him up. I looked at them both and laughed.

There was a nursery and primary school just along the road, and I was lucky enough to be able to get him straight in on regular sessions. This would allow me to carry on working with his routine being interrupted. Although they said they didn't mind, it also meant that I didn't have to rely on my mother and Aunt Linda for baby sitting duties.

Aunt Linda h given the go ahead to mum with taking Cameron on holiday with them, on the provision that I sorted out the trouble with Epic Security. And of course, I promised that it would all be over by the time they returned. I drove through to the passport office at Durham and spent an arm and a leg getting him a passport processed through the fast track system.

My first session of the day wasn't until eleven o'clock, so I decided to have a bit of a lie in. My angel of a mother had previously agreed to get up early with Cameron and sort him out with breakfast before taking him to nursery. I did actually hear Cameron wake up at about half six, but it felt great being able to turn over in my lovely warm bed and drift back off to sleep.

Approximately half an hour later, I was rudely awoken by my mother shouting up the stairs for me.

"Mark. You'd better come down and see this, son!" she yelled.

I threw on a pair of shorts and ran downstairs to see what was so important. Mother was stood at the open front door, looking out.

"What's up?" I asked.

"It's your van, son." she replied without looking at me.

I peered out to see that my van had been covered in bright red paint, and all four tyres had been slashed. The letters "EB" were deeply etched into the bonnet, which made it painfully obvious who was responsible

My blood had instantly reached boiling point and my fists were clenched. I was ready to explode.

"Have you booked your holiday yet, mam?" I asked through gritted teeth.

"Aye son," she replied, "we go tomorrow night. Why?"

"Any chance you and Cameron can stay round Aunty Linda's until then?" I continued.

"We could, Mark, but I'll need to get a shifty on with the packing. You'll have to help with packing Cameron's things." mum said.

"Of course I will, mam," I said, "Unfortunately, things a re going to get a bit heated around here, and I think it would be best if you and the boy were out the way, if you know what I mean."

After helping mum with the packing and giving Cameron something to eat, I ordered a taxi to pick them up and take then over to Aunt Linda's house.

I waved them off as they drove away, and then I went back into the house and grabbed the telephone. After telling Jez, Nick and Lurch what had happened, I asked them to come over to the house as soon as they could, and to be prepared to stay over for a couple of days. I also rang Lucy to say that I wasn't feeling well, and that I was closing the unit for the rest of the week. I asked her to pop into work in the morning and reschedule any classes that were already booked for the week.

Nick and Lurch arrived first, and they appeared to be prepared for a week long piss up. They each carried a small rucksack with spare clothes and toiletries, but they were both buckling under the weight of all the beer crates they were struggling to carry.

"Jesus Christ" Where the fuck are you two going?" I asked

"Well we had to stock up on the essentials mate. You did say we were staying over for a couple of days." Nick replied with a smile.

"As long as it's not some sort of scout's camping trip you're expecting." I said.

Once Jez turned up, we sorted out the sleeping arrangements, and then took one of the beer crates out into the back garden. Nick placed the crate in the middle of the patio table, tore open the cellophane wrapping and handed us each a can.

"Right lads," I began, "First thing's first. All of you do me a favour, and please don't get too shit faced. I want to pop out later tonight for a bit of snooping around before we get the ball rolling tomorrow."

"So what's the sketch, Mark?" Lurch asked.

"What's going to happen is," I began, "I'm going to pop down to Hylton Castle and have a look about Eric Barnes' place. I want to know my way around before tomorrow. So Jez, if you don't mind, I'd like you to come with me tonight."

I waited for Jez's nod of acknowledgement, and then switched my attention to Nick and Lurch.

"While we're out, I want you two to keep an eye on this place. So far I've had a brick through my window and my van trashed outside, so I wouldn't be surprised if anything else happens. But if anyone's creeping around here, I want them to think that I'm up and about. And whatever you do, do not leave the house unattended, unless the place is burning to the fucking ground. Hopefully, me and Jez should only be gone a couple of hours, anyway."

"Well in that case mate," Jez said, "I won't bother having any more beer until we get back. That way, I can drive there and back. I'm not fucking walking all that way!"

"No problems, Jez." I said laughing.

Nick took a huge gulp from his beer, then asked, "So what's happening tomorrow, Mark?"

I took a few sips from my beer, and then continued with the plan, "I think the reason why Eric knows so much about me is because of Clive. So we need to get him out of the picture. First thing in the morning, we'll go down to Castletown and invite him back here for a little chat. I've got a few questions for him. Are you okay with using your car for that, Jez?"

"Yes mate," he replied, "Just as long as we don't make it obvious to everyone that we're fucking kidnapping someone. Oh, and don't get any blood on my upholstery."

"Good," I continued, "We'll all go down to get Clive, and while he's here, one of us can stay with him at all times, just in case he decides to get a bit brave. Then we'll pay a visit to Eric's office, and give him something to remember, and make sure he doesn't fucking bother any of us again. Just to let you know lads, I'm not fucking around any more I want these bastards to know that I mean business when it comes to my family, and if they play with fire they're going to get burned." Now you might already know this, but it's rumoured that these lot might be tooled up, so we can't afford to hang around. We need to get in and strike before they even get the chance to react.

After a long debate, it was decided that we would order some pizzas. When our food arrived, we placed it on the patio table, and we tucked in. The whole lot was demolished within minutes. Feeling full, I went back into the house and collapsed on the sofa. The boys followed suit, and the four of us slouched, saying nothing.

"Eventually, Nick stood up and said, "Well, if we're going to do nowt but sit about for now, I might as well pop a DVD on for us to watch."

"Aye, good idea mate," I said, "As long as it's not one of those weird animal porn movies you're into."

We were all laughing, apart from Nick. He gave me a two fingered gesture as he left the room to get his bag. A few minutes later, he walked back in with a small selection of DVDs. He threw them on my lap and sat back down. I picked one out, a comedy as we could do with a laugh, and placed it into the machine.

Nick and Jez had fallen asleep within minutes of the movie starting, and I was beginning to feel a bit sleepy. Just so I wouldn't doze off, I walked out to the back garden and lit up a cigarette. I sat at the patio table and grabbed what was left of my beer and guzzled the lot until it was empty. Lurch came out and sat opposite me and asked for a cigarette.

"You shouldn't smoke you know mate," I said, "It'll stunt your growth apparently."

"Oh well," he replied jokingly, "I'll have to smoke about a hundred a day for the next twenty years to get down to your size then, short arse,"

There was a slight pause before Lurch spoke again, "You okay, Mark mate?"

"No, not really Lurch," I replied, "A mixed bag of emotions at the moment, mate. I'm fucking angry, scared and rather excited too."

"You're excited? What the bloody hell you all excited about?" he asked.

"I know this might sound a bit daft, mate. But I get a bit of an adrenalin rush out of all this." I replied again.

Lurch shook his head in disbelief and said, "You're definitely warped in that fucking head of yours mate. I'm fucking shitting myself."

I looked at Lurch and smiled, "It's only natural Lurch,

don't worry. But if you're totally uncomfortable about getting too involved, I'd understand."

"Oh I know I don't have to get involved," he replied, "But I want to. I'm not letting any twats do my mates over. Not only that, you've done plenty for me in the past. So don't worry about it."

"What about Nick then?" I asked.

"Oh he's filling his pants as well, but he's the same as me. He'll do anything for a good mate." he answered.

"Aye," I continued, "he might act a bit of an arsehole now again, and I know he loves winding the shit out of you, Lurch. But his heart's in the right place, and he is a good mate."

Lurch and I went back into the living room where Jez and Nick were snoring their heads off. Lurch dropped onto the sofa next to Nick, and I could see he was feeling tired. I decided that Jez and I would pay a visit to Eric's place at about two in the morning, just to ensure no one is around then. I looked at my watch and it was only half eight in the evening. I set the alarm on my watch to go off at midnight, and I sat on the sofa next to Jez and drifted off to sleep.

I woke up after what seemed like an eternity, but when I checked my watch it was only twenty past ten. I still had over an hour and a half yet to go. The boys weren't in the living room, so I wondered if it was them that made me wake up. Bet they're in the back garden getting pissed.

I walked through the kitchen and out the back door into the garden. No one was around. Now this was strange. As I walked back into the living room, scratching my head, I heard footsteps upstairs. The cheeky buggers have gone to bed! They'll never get up at midnight now, and even if they do they'll feel like shit. I slowly crept up the stairs. I loved the element of surprise.

As I got to the top of the stairs I noticed that my bedroom door was slightly ajar, and I could hear voices inside. I swung the door open and my eyes popped out of my head with what I saw.

Sandra was knelt on all fours on my bed. In front and behind her were the two officers I had previously put in hospital, and they were doing exactly what they were before. Had they not learned from their mistakes? I filled with rage and screamed.

The alarm made me jump out of the sofa, but it was my screams that really woke up Jez, Nick and Lurch.
"What the fuck was that?" Nick yelled.
"Erm sorry lads," I apologised, "Think I've just had one of my freaky dreams again."
"Shit, man," Jez added, "You gave me the shock of my fucking life. Think the sooner we get this sorted, the sooner you get your head back together."
While the lads were still busy waking up and getting over the shock of their wake up call, I went into the kitchen and made four strong cups of coffee. I took them into the dining room and placed them on the table.
"There you go lads. Stop scratching you balls, and get this down your necks. These should help to wake you up. And make the most of it, because I don't know when you'll get time for another one. It's all go in about two hours time." I told them.
I went back into the kitchen and knocked up a few bacon sandwiches, and the lads' faces lit up when I brought them through to the dining room. Within minutes, the coffees and sandwiches were gone, and we were all raring to go.
Jez grabbed his car keys, and before we left, I reminded Nick and Lurch about what to do and what not to do if anything happened.
We drove down to Hylton Castle, and I got Jez to park the car on the main road rather than in the empty car park which was directly opposite the shops and office. We walked along past the shops until we reached the office door, but the motion sensors that set off the security lights gave us the incentive to move on. We

carried on along the shops until we reached the end where there was an alleyway leading around to the rear of the shops. We eventually came across a solid wooden door which had a similar plaque to the front door with "Epic Security Company" and Eric's name engraved onto it. Jez checked to see if the door was locked. It wasn't locked, but the second we opened it, a blinding security light beamed down onto us. I needed to get into that office without being noticed.

I reached into the inside pocket of my jacket, and pulled out my "Black Widow" catapult. I placed a ball bearing in the pouch and asked Jez to open the door again. I aimed the catapult in the general direction of the light, and pulled back the thick elastic. Almost immediately after releasing the elastic, there was the sound of breaking glass and we were sent into pitch darkness. Perfect.

We stood in a corner of the yard for a few moments, anticipating the sound of breaking glass alerting someone. Nothing. I looked up the long wooden stair case that lead to the rear office door and noticed their was quite a large glass panel in the middle of it. I whispered to Jez to wait at the bottom of the stairs until I got the door open, then sprinted up and crouched down to make myself less visible. I slipped my leather gloves on, stood up and put my fist through the window, then crouched down again in case I had alerted anyone again. Still nothing. I reached through the window and unlocked the door from the inside, and the door swung open. I signalled down to Jez for him to come and join me. We both walked in and quietly closed the door behind us.

On the wall at the other end of the corridor was an alarm system control box, and thankfully there appeared to be no lights flashing on it. To the left was a door which lead into a small store room, and when I peered in I found the main electricity box. I opened the main cover to switch off the mains supply. Jez then ran along the corridor to the alarm box, grabbed the wiring loom that went into it and yanked it until the wires were loose in his hand.

Jez faced down the corridor towards me, and waved for me to come and see. He pointed to a door on his left that was slightly ajar. I peered in to look at what appeared to be the main office that Eric used. We walked into the small room and closed the door behind us. The street lamps outside were emitting sufficient light into the office window so there was no need for us to use torches. There was a four drawer filing cabinet in the far left corner of the room, so I made a bee line towards that while Jez searched through the desk drawers. We were looking for any incriminating evidence to prove that Eric was indeed a dodgy, dangerous twat.

"Hmm, I wonder if he's got a licence for this." Jez said as he revealed a pistol in one of the desk drawers.

"Give me that, mate. I'll check to see if it's loaded or made ready before you put it in your pocket. Don't want you blowing your knackers off, do we?" I said, quietly laughing.

Jez carefully handed me the gun, and I pressed the release button on the pistol grip allowing the magazine to drop into my free hand. I passed the magazine over to Jez, and then pulled back the working parts of the pistol to check inside the chamber for any unspent rounds. It was clear. I let go of the mechanism and fired off the action, and then finally handed the weapon over to Jez.

I carried on searching through the filing cabinet until I came across a folder that had names and addresses filled out in a table. Next to each name was a column titled "amount owed" and a column for "amount paid". Some of the letters had a letter "V" written next to them, but I couldn't figure out what it meant. I pulled out some of the pages from the file, rolled them up and placed them into my jacket pocket.

"Right mate," I whispered to Jez, "I think we've got enough to play with now. Let's get out of here."

We both came out of the office and ran along the corridor to the back door. I opened it slightly and peered my head out to check that the coast was clear. It didn't look like we had attracted any attention, so we ran down the wooden stairs, though the yard and out the gate. We continued running down the back alley until we reached the main road where we had parked the car.

As we both sat in the car, we looked at each other and began laughing like a pair of naughty school boys who had just robbed a sweet shop. Come to think of it, that was quite easy. Too easy, in fact.

Jez started up the car, and we headed back home.

Chapter 13

Nick and Lurch were, shockingly, still wide awake when we got back from Eric's office.

"Everything okay, lads?" I asked as I walked into the living room.

"Aye, it's been quiet mate. No problems what so ever." Lurch replied.

"You and Jez fancy a cuppa, or how about something a bit stronger?" Nick asked as he walked into the kitchen.

"Oh please," Jez replied as he flopped onto the sofa, "But sod the coffee, grab me a beer."

Nick came back into the room with four beers, and we all sat and guzzled until the cans were empty.

Lurch placed his can on the floor by his feet and asked, "So how did it go then? You find anything?"

"Funny you should mention that," Jez replied, "I've found this little beauty."

He pulled out the pistol from his pocket and placed it on the floor, and then put the magazine next to it. Lurch's and Nick's eyes almost popped out their heads. I picked up the magazine and emptied the rounds into my hand. There were ten of them. I refilled the magazine, picked up the pistol and put them both in the drawer on the television cabinet. The paperwork I nabbed from the office was passed around the lads, and none of them could make sense of the letter "V" that was written by some of the names. I decided that after we had been to collect Clive, I would make a few phone calls to try and figure it out.

After another couple of hours of broken sleep, some

breakfast and copious amounts of coffee, the four of us got into Jez's car and drove down to Castletown. We drove into Jennifer Avenue and parked at the end of the street. I asked Nick and Lurch to come with me, and Jez to stay at the bottom of the street until we had gotten into the house. I told him that as soon as we entered the house, he was to drive up to the door and wait for us. The three of us walked up to Clive's house and Nick and Lurch stood against the wall so they were out of sight from whoever answered the door.

I tapped lightly on the door, and after a few moments, Clive answered. Without saying a word, I kicked the door wide open, pinning Clive to the wall, and Nick and Lurch followed me in.

As Lurch slammed the door shut behind him, I got Clive into a head lock, dragged him into the living room and threw him to the floor. There was a look of utter terror on Clive's face as he cowered on the floor looking at the three of us.

"What the fuck you playing at? What do you want?" he screamed nervously.

"First of all, you jumped up little prick. I want you to keep your fucking gob shut, because we don't want to be waking the neighbours do we? And if you don't, I'll shut you up permanently." I warned him.

I went down on one knee by Clive's side and I slammed my fist into his face twice, knocking him out cold. I then rolled him onto his back, and pulling a handful of cable ties out of my pocket, I tied his hands behind his back.

Lurch and Nick picked Clive up and placed him on the sofa. Then Lurch pulled out a roll of duct tape to cover his eyes and mouth. God, that's going to hurt when I pull it off, slowly.

I asked Nick to run out to make sure that Jez was by the front door, and asked him to open the boot before we came out. Lurch and I picked up Clive by his arms and dragged him out of the living room and along the corridor to the front door. Nick was stood outside by the rear of the car with the boot open. As soon as we got Clive out the door, Nick grabbed his legs to help lift the dead weight into the boot. I slammed it shut and we all got into the car.

Jez reversed his car onto the drive of my house, and I got out to let Nick and Lurch in. I walked through the kitchen, into the back garden and opened the side gate so we could bring Clive into the house without looking too suspicious. Jez opened the boot, and the four of us dragged the semi conscious Clive out and into the back garden. While I locked the side gate, the others took Clive into the living room. I placed one of the dining chairs in the middle of the living room, and we sat Clive on his chair, tying his hands to it so he couldn't move. As Clive wasn't quite with us yet, I asked Nick to make some coffees for us all, and we sat on the sofas drinking while we looked at the pathetic excuse of a man tied up in the middle of the room.

Drinking the last few drops from my cup, I stood up and said, "Well, we haven't got all day, so let's say hello to Clivey boy."

I lifted Clive's head up by his chin, and slapped him hard across his face.

"Good morning lover boy. Wakey wakey!" I shouted.

For a few seconds, Clive shuffled about on his seat but soon realised he was going nowhere, and eventually settled.

"Right Clive," I said to him, "I'm going to take off you blindfold and your gag. Now if you so much as let out a whimper, I'll give you something to moan about."

Clive muffled a "yes" and nodded his head.

I gently pulled away at a corner of the tape that covered his eyes, then ripped it off, making Clive let out a muffled scream. The lads laughed as they noticed that parts of Clive's eyebrows had come off and were stuck to the tape. There was also a pale rectangular patch had removed some of his fake tan. I then quickly removed the tape from his mouth, almost ripping his lips off. Wow! This tape was good stuff!

I sat on the edge of the sofa facing Clive and waited for him to recover from the tape removal, and as he looked up at me, I could see tears rolling down his face.

"Oh what's up sweetheart?" I asked with sarcasm, "Did the nasty man hurt you?"

"You won't get away with this, Mark," he said through his tears, "Just wait until Eric finds out what you've done. He'll fucking kill you."

I slowly stood up, slapped Clive across the face again, and then sat back down on the sofa.

"I'm one step ahead of you Clive, you fuckwit." I said, "I already know that you work for him. That's how he knows so much about me isn't it? You've been letting your fucking mouth go, haven't you?"

"What the hell you going on about?" he asked me.

"Well, sweetheart," I started to explain, "How else would he know where I live, where I work, and even know my fucking mother's name? No one threatens my family! You've let your fucking mouth go, Clive, and do you really think I should let you get away with that?"

"I haven't said anything to anyone." he exclaimed.

"I've got some news for you, sunshine, and it's all bad. I don't fucking believe you." I said, "And on top of that, I don't fucking like you anyway. I've heard the way you spoke to my son, and how do I know that you haven't raised your hands to him?"

Clive shook his head, and now looked very afraid, "No, I wouldn't so that. I'm not like that."

"Again, I don't believe you Clive," I said, "You're nothing but a toe rag, who works for an even bigger toe rag. Now I think I need to show you what being in pain is all about. I'm going to make sure that the likes of you, and the rest of the brainless monkeys you work with, no longer make other people's lives a fucking misery. You make money from bullying other people, don't you Clive?"

Before he could try and fee me any more bullshit, I walked over to where my jacket was hanging in the hallway, and came back with the paperwork that I stole from Eric's office.

I waved the paperwork in his face and said, "I've got a list of names here and it shows that people owe Eric money."

Clive looked at me arrogantly and replied, "Yeah, and?"

I unrolled one of the sheets and put it in front of his face to read. I pointed at one of the names and said, "Tell me why some of these names have the letter "V" next to them."

He looked at the page, then looked at me and shrugged his shoulders, pleading ignorance.

I stood up in front of him and demanded, "Why is there a "V" next to some of the names?"

I slammed my fist into his face to give him some incentive into answering my questions.

"I will ruin that fucking pretty face of yours if you don't start talking and give me the answers I want. Trust me Clive, if you don't play the game, you won't be walking out of here. You'll be carried out on a fucking stretcher." I warned him.

"For God's sake," he began, "That's a list of who owes Eric money. If there's a V next to a name, it means that they haven't paid what they owe, and Eric sends someone to pay them a visit."

"So not only does he run a protection racquet, but he's a fucking loan shark as well! Oh this is getting better." I said with a warped smile emerging on my face.

I was about to give Clive another slap when the telephone rang. As I was walking into the hallway to answer it, I asked Jez to put another gag on Clive. I picked up the phone and walked into the kitchen to take the call.

The voice on the other end of the line said, "Hello, I'm PC Lomas, I'd like to speak to a Mister Harrison please."

"Yep, speaking." I replied.

"Hello Mister Harrison," the policeman continued, "I've been dealing with the case of your wife's accident, and I was wondering if you cold possible come down to the station for a quick chat."

"Why, what's up?" I asked.

"No, there's nothing for you to worry about. I've just got some information for you, and I would rather talk to you face to face, if that's okay." he said.

"Well, I'm kind of in the middle of something at the moment. Can it wait?" I asked.

"I'd rather speak to you sooner rather than later. It'll only take a few minutes hopefully. Like I said, I've got some information for you, and it's quite important." he went on.

"Erm, okay then. I'll come down as soon as I can mate. Just give me half and hour or so." I said.

"Not a problem, Mister Harrison," the policeman said, "Just come to the main reception and ask for me, PC Lomas. I'll be waiting for you."

I placed the phone back on it's docking station and walked back into the living room. Everyone was looking at me with a puzzled expression.

"It's okay lads, nothing to worry about." I reassured them, "That was just the police who've been dealing with Sandra's death. They want me to pop down because they've got some information for me or something."

"So what shall we do here then, mate?" Lurch asked.

"Well I should only be an hour or so. So if you lot just stay here, and keep an eye on lover boy here until I get back. If he tried getting brave or sets his lip up, just slap him about a bit. He doesn't bite." I replied.

Jez let me borrow his car, seems as my van was temporarily out of action. So I drove down to the station to find out what was going on.

PC Lomas came to the reception and invited me into one

of the small interview rooms. We both sat at a small desk, and he placed a file in front of him and opened it.

After reading through some of the file, he looked up at me and asked, "Do you know if your wife had any enemies, or if she had upset anyone?"

"Hmm, not that I know of. I mean, we weren't exactly best of friends, but we were getting there." I replied.

"Well, her car has been checked over, and it appears that someone had tampered with her braking system. The brake pipes had been cut." he said.

"You're fucking kidding!" I exclaimed, "I thought she was just drunk."

"The results did show that she was well over the limit," he continued, "but the main cause of the accident was the fact that her brakes failed."

It was obvious that this was Eric's doing, but I didn't want to say anything. Especially with the fact that I had recently burgled his office and I had one of his boys tied up back at my house.

"I'm totally shocked mate," I said, "I'm absolutely gob smacked, and wish I knew what to say. If I could help, I would, but I can't think of anyone who would do this sort of thing."

"Okay, Mister Harrison. Thank you." the policeman said, ""That's all I wanted you for. If I receive any more information I will get back to you. And if you hear anything, please don't hesitate to let me know."

I stood up and shook the policeman's hand, then left the station to go back home. I had some unfinished business to deal with.

When I got back home, I went straight into the living room and asked Lurch if he would be kind enough to make us all a cup of coffee.

Clive was watching my every move from his chair, and

when I looked closer, I noticed blood dripping into his eyes and tape over his mouth.

"You been upsetting my friends, lover boy?" I asked him.

"No mate," Jez answered, "We just fancied a bit fun with the duct tape. We had a go to see how many strips of tape it would take to completely remove his eyebrows.

"Well it's certainly done the fucking job, mate." I laughed.

"Ha, it only took four strips, and one of them was for his mouth," Jez added, "We had to gag him because he was screaming like a fucking girl. It's good shit that tape mind. Took his skin off, never mind his hair. I don't think they'll be growing back for a while."

I grabbed Clive by his chin to force eye contact with me and asked him, "You feeling scared, Clivey boy?"

His muffled response made no sense, so I tore the tape from his mouth, making him squeal like a little pig. His lips were now red and very swollen, and looked like they were ready to burst open.

"Well, here's something to really cause you concern, sunshine." I said, "Sandra's crash wasn't an accident. Your fucking bouncer buddies thought it would be a good idea to snip her brake pipes. You think they did that to get at me, do you?"

He opened his mouth to say something, but before he had the opportunity, I gave him a right hook, sending his head spinning, and blood spattering from his face.

"You honestly think I give a shit about that slag?" I asked him, "The only thing that's boiling my piss, is that my boy could've been in that car. Who the hell do you lot think you are?"

I was winding myself up, and I could feel the rage build up inside me. My fists were clenched so hard, it looked like my knuckles looked like they were about to burst through the skin. I looked at Clive, covered in blood and looking rather pathetic. I had no pity for him. I was just angry and frustrated.

I grabbed Clive by the throat with my left hand, and

squeezed hard as I repeatedly pounded my right fist into his face. His head moved back and forth as my fist pummelled into him, and I could feel my anger and frustration release with every punch.

Jez grabbed me from behind and pulled me back, "Fucking hell Mark, You'll kill him!" he shouted at me.

I stood there, breathing heavily and looked at Clive, and I felt nothing but hatred. I did actually feel like killing him.

Lurch came back into the room and almost dropped the coffee cups when he saw the state of Clive.

"Jesus, mate." he said, "Remind me never to piss you off."

I dropped onto the sofa and looked at the lads, and then said, "Sandra's brake pipes were cut. That's why she crashed. And I bet you can work out who did it."

"Ah, bollocks mate," Lurch said, "I don't know what to say. What do you want to do now then?"

I leaned forward and put my head in my hands, thinking. After clearing my head, I stood up and walked around the room, then eventually came to a stand still in front of Clive.

"Right," I began, "Nick, if you can stay here and keep an eye on what's left of Clive. Make sure he doesn't try anything. Not that I think he's in a fit state to do anything anyway. Jez and Lurch, if you two can come with me. We're going to pay a little visit to Eric's office. If he's not in, we'll fucking wait for him. I just want the two of you there in case things get a bit heavy."

"What are we going to do when we actually get there though, mate?" Jez asked.

"Hopefully, I'm just going to have a heated debate with Mister fucking Barnes, and get him to back off. And if he doesn't, I'll rip his fucking throat out."

"And if things get nasty?" Jez asked again.

"Well he can't shoot me, so what's the worse he can do? I'm sure that, between the three of us, we can handle any of his monkeys that might try it on. And Eric's just an old has been. I'll pull his head off and shit down his neck if he even takes a step towards me." I replied.

"Fair enough," Jez commented, "right then, shall we get this over and done with?

"Ha, I want my cuppa first. Can't do anything without another caffeine fix." I said.

We left the car in the car park in front of Eric's office. I wanted the car close this time. Just in case we needed a quick get away. As I got out the car, I zipped up my jacket and checked the baton I had slipped up my left sleeve. Jez hid a short stumpy length of pool cue up his sleeve too.

We walked over to the office building and as I opened the door, I noticed that the place was quiet. Very quiet, actually. I signalled for Jez and Lurch to be quiet as we climbed the stairs. Once at the top, I slowly opened the door and peered my head round to find the place was empty. Strange, why would the place be empty, but open? Directly ahead of us was Eric's office, and the door was slightly ajar. This didn't feel right, as all that was missing was an invitation for us. I slowly opened the door, and once we were all in the office, I closed it behind us.

"Mark, come and look at this." Lurch whispered.

There was a laptop computer on the desk with a note stuck to it. Two words were scribbled on the note - "press return". I looked at Lurch and Jez then opened up the compute and pressed the return button.

The computer's media player flashed up, and I could just make out a deliberately distorted image of a man sitting at this very desk. I moved the cursor onto the "play" button to listen to the message.

"Hello there Mister Harrison, I bet this is a bit of a surprise for you, isn't it? I came into my office this morning and noticed that someone had broken into it. Although you were quite vigilant during your little operation, you failed to notice the

CCTV cameras I have dotted around the place. You're quite an impressive little cat burglar, aren't you?

I don't take kindly to people snooping around in my business, and you have something of importance belonging to me. I want that paperwork back Mister Harrison, and I want it now. As an insurance, I now have something belonging to you. Lucy is a lovely young girl, and the boys have informed me that she's up for almost anything, after a bit of persuasion, that is. Feisty little thing she is, apparently. Bit young for me though.

So here's the deal. You give me my paperwork back, and you can have your sexy little secretary back in more or less one piece. We will be waiting for you inside the castle and Hylton Dene tonight, and you've got until ten o'clock to show your face. Come along with the paperwork, by yourself, and we will do a swap.

I gather you're an intelligent man, Mister Harrison, and that you will want this to run smoothly. You don't want Lucy to get hurt do you? You will get what you want, when I get what I want. See you tonight."

The distorted image faded and was replaced by a clear photograph of Lucy. She was tied and gagged, sitting in a dark corner. I couldn't quite make out where she was, but I could see that she had been knocked about a bit, by the blood smeared over her face, and her clothes were torn and dirty.

I switched the computer off and handed it over to Jez, saying, "We'll keep hold of this mate, might come in handy."

"So what the fuck are we going to do now, Mark? The bastards have got Lucy!" Jez asked.

"Well I can't afford to fuck about," I replied, "I'm just going to have to give in to Eric and hand over his paperwork. I don't want Lucy coming to any harm."

"Let's get out of here then, and get back home." Lurch suggested.

As I walked out of the office, a fist came flying out of

nowhere, and landed square on my face. Jez and Lurch ran out of the office and jumped onto the suited heavy, bringing him crashing to the floor. By the time I had shaken myself together, the man was laid out on the floor, and Jez and Lurch were sorting themselves out.

"The cheeky fucker!" I said, "I bet he was supposed to stay here and let Eric know that I've been. The dozy twat obviously couldn't resist having a pop at us. Good job he punches like a bitch."

I searched his pockets, and pulled out a mobile phone, a knuckle duster and a wallet. I then pulled off his tie and got the boys to drag him into the bathroom along the corridor. After struggling to lift the heavy lump onto the toilet seat, I used his tie to secure him to the pipes behind him. He was going nowhere. I then stuffed a handful of toilet paper into the man's mouth to gag him.

"Right," I said, "As you suggested before we were rudely interrupted, let's get the fuck out of here."

When we got back to the house, I asked Nick if he could pop into the kitchen and make us all something quick to eat while I went upstairs to my room. I pulled out an old army holdall from under my bed and threw it on top. In the bag was an old combat jacket, trousers and boots. I placed them to one side at the foot of the bed and looked to see what else I had stashed away. I found three thunder flashes, an old smoke grenade and a rusty old bayonet from an SA80 rifle, so I stuffed them into the combat jacket pockets, and brought the jacket, trousers and boots downstairs with me. Downstairs, I added the mobile phone, knuckle duster and wallet to the paraphernalia in my jacket pockets.

Clive was still tied up in the same spot, but his head was resting on his chest.

I shouted through to the kitchen, "Hey Nick, have you

killed him with your cooking or something?"

"Ha, not mate, think he's just sleeping. I was going to put a pillowcase over his head, because I was sick of looking at his ugly mug, but I didn't want to chance getting any blood on your mam's bedding. She'd fucking kill me!" he replied.

Lurch and Jez were sat at the dining table, so I joined them, and after a few moments of awkward silence, Lurch finally spoke.

"This is getting a bit fucking heavy, by the way, mate." he said.

"Oh I know mate," I replied, "It's great isn't it?"

Jez began to laugh, "You really are warped, aren't you? I'd love to know what's going on inside that mashed up head of yours."

"Well when you find out mate," I continued, "Let me know because I haven't got a clue half the time either."

Nick came through carrying four cups of coffee. He placed them carefully on the table and then said, "The sausage butties are nearly done lads. Won't be long."

I grabbed Nick by his arm and ushered him to sit at the table with us.

"Come and sit down a minute mate," I said to him, "There's been a few developments, so I'll tell you what's going on."

I explained to Nick about the laptop, and Lucy being with Eric's boys. Then I went on to tell him about having to meet him later tonight.

"Oh, fucking marvellous," he said, "This just gets better, doesn't it?"

"Well Eric wants me to go on my own tonight, so there's not a lot more you lot can do. I'll be going there for about ten, so I want you three to hang fire back here. And if you don't hear from me by midnight, just ring the police. Jez, if you could drop me off later, then just come back here with Lurch and Nick." I said.

As Nick got back up to go into the kitchen, I noticed Clive beginning to stir. I got up and walked over to where he was slumped in his chair.

"Look at me, you fucking prick!" I ordered him.

Clive's head slowly lifted upwards towards me, and he stared at me through his swollen bloodied eyes. When he smiled, I noticed that I must have knocked out his front teeth, and blood poured out of his mouth down his chin. He looked a mess.

Clive gave me a weak bloody grin as he said, "You honestly think you're going to walk away from all of this?" You're going to be carried away in a wooden jacket, mate. They'll fucking kill you!"

I gave him another right hook, to remind him of the situation he was currently in. As he struggled to lift his head back up, I said to him, "First of all sunshine. I'm not your fucking mate. And secondly, do you think I'm scared of a load of cardboard gangsters? Eric's a has been, and you and the rest of your fuckwits are just wannabes. You're all probably hard as nails when you're all together in your pride, but let's face it. You haven't got a brain cell between you all. And when you're not in your little gaggle, none of you could fight your way out of a wet paper bag."

Clive shook his head and began to laugh, so I punched him again, knocking him unconscious yet again.

I looked over to Jez and Lurch and said, "This twat just doesn't know when to shut the fuck up does he?

It was coming up to half past nine, so I took my things upstairs, and got myself ready. Once my combats and boots were on, I rearranged everything in my pockets, and slid my telescopic baton up my left sleeve. I then went downstairs, and when I walked into the living room, the lads just stared at me, bewildered.

"Fucking hell!" Jez exclaimed, "Mark's gone all Rambo on us, lads."

"You planning the next world war or something, mate?"

Nick asked.

"I just like to be well prepared in situations like this. I know for a fact that this ain't going to be plain sailing when I get there, so I need to expect the unexpected." I replied.

I checked over my pockets one more time, and then nodded to Jez.

"Right mate. I'm ready when you are." I said, "Grab your car keys, and let's do this."

I turned my attention to the other two and continued issuing my orders, "Nick and Lurch, stay here and keep an eye on Clivey boy until I get back. Hopefully I'll be back in about two hours in time for tea and medals."

Lurch came over to me, and wrapped one of his long arms around me and pulled me in towards himself, "Good luck mate, and be bloody careful."

"Thanks mate," I said, "I think I'm going to need it."

Chapter 14

Not much was said in the car between Jez and I on the way down to Hylton Dene. I think he was more nervous than me. We turned right onto Washington Road, and I asked him to pull over at the bus stop opposite the castle grounds. I wanted to walk around to the entrance rather than risking Eric seeing me being dropped off and thinking I'm not alone.

As I got out the car I patted Jez on the shoulder and told him to go back home. And as previously discussed, I told him to ring the police if I wasn't back by midnight.

Once Jez pulled away, I walked across the road and around the corner, leading to the entrance gate to the castle. The gates were locked, so I quickly climbed over them, and when I landed on the other side, I crouched down behind a tree to take a moment to compose myself. After a couple of deep breaths, I stepped out from behind the tree and began slowly walking towards the castle along the gravel path.

If it wasn't for the bright moonlight, I would've been in total darkness, and the gigantic castle in front of me would've just been a huge shadow. The gravel path snaked along towards the main entrance of the castle, and over in the distance, to the left of the castle, I could just make out the outline of Saint Catherine's chapel. It was a lot smaller than the castle itself, but looked just as disconcerting in the dark. Huge trees were scattered around the grounds, and as I walked along the gravel path, I noticed the old grave stone that belongs to the legendary "Cauld Lad". This place was creepy.

As I approached where the pathway opened out and spread across the full width of the castle, I saw a figure appear from behind a tree and slowly walk towards me. I stopped and allowed the figure to come to me. My fists were clenched and ready to go.

The figure stopped two or three metres away from me and a voice came from it.

"I assume you're Mister Harrison." the voice said.

"Depends who's asking." I replied.

"Well I'm Eric Barnes, and I do believe you've come here to hand something over to me." the voice rasped.

"Not so fast, Barnes." I said, "You'll get your paperwork when I know Lucy's okay, and she's with me. Where is she?"

"She's in the castle, entertaining some of my boys," he said mockingly, "Give me the paperwork, and you can have your secretary back."

I took a few steps closer to Eric, until I could just make out his facial features and said, "You're either deaf or fucking plain stupid, because I've just said that you'll get your paperwork when I get Lucy. And trust me when I say that if she's come to any harm, I will drop on you like a ton of shit."

"Now now, Mister Harrison," he continued to mock, "You're not really in a position to dish out any threats. Lucy's in the castle, so if you want her, I suggest you go and get her. I'll be waiting here for you to come back with the paperwork. And remember, my boys are looking forward to meeting you."

I reached into one of my jacket pockets, pulled out the wallet belonging to the man back at Eric's place, and threw it at Eric.

"Well if that twat's anything to go by," it was my turn to mock, "I'm not going to have much of a problem am I?"

Eric threw the wallet onto the floor and laughed, "For some strange reason, Mister Harrison, I like you. You've got guts. But tonight, you're bravery could be your downfall. Like I said, if you want Lucy, go and get her."

I began walking towards the castle entrance, and as I passed Eric, I made sure that our shoulders brushed, putting some considerable force behind it to send him back a little. Without looking back, I said to Eric, "Now you wait here, old man, I'll be coming back for you."

When I reached the castle gate, I paused and looked back. Eric was stood watching me, but he was now on his mobile phone. No doubt he was warning his monkeys inside the castle that I was on my way.

The lock on the enormous heavy wooden door had been broken off and was slightly open. I peered through to see that the whole place was dimly lit by strip lights. Before entering, I pulled out my telescopic baton, and flicked it out to it's full extent, then I stepped through the door. Directly opposite to where I was standing was a small archway that lead to a dark spiral staircase going up to the upper floors. To my left was a large unused dried up well with an iron grid covering it. A stone wall, standing approximately two feet tall, ran the full length of the room, apart from a gap in the middle. I assumed that his wall originally partitioned the ground floor into several rooms, but had slowly eroded in time. I looked up to the left and noticed a window on each of the other two floors. Dim lights flickered out of both rooms, but I could not hear anything yet.

I crept down the stone steps and walked over to the right to the small wall. I crouched down behind the wall and took the mobile phone out of my jacket pocket. There were dozens of names in the phones contacts menu, and I randomly rang some of them, until I came across the name "Oz". I pressed the button to ring Oz's number, and within seconds I could hear a high pitched ring come from the room from the third floor of the castle. Before the call was answered, I hung up. At least I knew where to go for Lucy, and at least I knew that Eric wasn't bluffing when he said his boys were here too.

Apart from scaling the inside of the caste walls, the only way to get to these rooms was to use the spiral staircase on the far side of the castle. Although the meat heads upstairs already probably already know I'm here, I still intended to achieve some sort of element of surprise, so I crawled along to the far right of the castle using the wall as cover. To remain out of the line of sight from the rooms above, I then crept around the outside edge of the ground floor until I reached the opening of the staircase.

With my back to the outer wall, I slowly walked up the stairs until I could see the opening to the first room. I dropped to my knees and slowly made my way to the opening on all fours. I poked my head around the doorway at floor level for a fraction of a second, but long enough to take everything in. there were three heavies at the far side of the long empty room. They were huddled around a small wooden box playing cards, and not one of them were facing the opening. Ideal.

As I couldn't see Lucy, I assumed that she was in the next room above, but before I begin world war three, I need to know how many more men I may have to deal with, and the exact location and state of Lucy. So I took one more peep around the doorway, and the three muscle brains were still enthralled in their game of snap. I jumped up the three stairs to clear me of the doorway, and I put my back against the wall again and paused, anticipating being heard. No one came out of the room, and when I had one last peek into the room, the three stooges were still concentrating on their game. Some fucking use they are!

The knuckle duster I acquired earlier was a snug fit on my left hand, and I also kept a tight grip on my baton in my right hand. My heart was now pounding, and I could feel the adrenalin rush around my body, making me tingle head to foot. I was struggling to control my breathing, and my chest was heaving as I felt a mixture of fear, excitement and apprehension run through my body.

As I slowly climbed the stairs, I heard a muffled cry come from the upper room. It was Lucy, and she sounded so distressed. Just as I neared the doorway I heard a dull thud, as if something had been thrown to the floor. I peered my head around the corner looking onto a room that was identical to the room below. Lucy was at the far end of the room, curled up in a foetal position in the corner. Her long blonder hair appeared to be dirty and matted. Her clothes were tattered and torn, and she wasn't wearing any shoes. She was also tied and gagged with thick rope.

Although my head was clearly sticking through the doorway, Lucy could not see me because of the man standing over her, causing her to cower in fear. He was the only man in there, meaning I only had four of them in total to deal with.

I walked into the room and crept up behind the man. Lucy glanced at me, and for a fraction of a second I could see a glimmer of hope in her eyes. I pursed my lips and signalled for her to stay silent.

Lucy closed her eyes, and curled up tightly into a ball, with her knees up by her face. I stamped my foot into the back of the man's right knee and he crashed to the ground. Before he had the chance to get back up or turn around, I got close up behind him and wrapped my right arm around his throat and held on with all my might. This man had some amazing strength and began throwing himself around the room, with me on his back. I reached around and grabbed my right elbow with my left hand, and pulled in tightly, restricting his breathing. This mountain of a man was not giving up, and was throwing me about on his back like a little rag doll, but I refused to let go.

After struggling for twenty seconds or so, he eventually slumped to the floor face down with me on top of him. My arms were throbbing from holding on so tightly for so long, and throughout the whole ordeal, I still managed to hold onto my baton.

As I picked myself up off the floor, Lucy looked up at me and I could see the relief in her eyes. I untied the rope from around her hands, and as soon as I had pulled the gag from her mouth, she threw her arms around me and hugged me like there was no tomorrow.

While she held onto me closely, I whispered in her ear, "Okay sweetheart, it's not over yet. We have to get out of here, and there's three other men downstairs. Just stay behind me until I say otherwise."

Before we left the room, I took out the smoke grenade from my jacket pocket, just in case, then we slowly made our way down the spiral stairs, until we reached the opening of the lower room where the henchmen were still busy playing cards. I could hear them muttering amongst themselves and as I peered my head around the door way, one of them turned and looked me straight in the eyes.

I grabbed Lucy's hand and shouted, "Run!"

The three men came stumbling out of the room after us as we flew down the stairs as fast as our legs could take us. I pulled the pin out of the smoke grenade and dropped it behind me. Within seconds, the staircase was filling with thick red smoke. I then ripped off the striker of the thunder flash and ignited it, and threw that up the stairs behind us. Just as we reached the archway at the bottom of the stairs there was an ear drum rupturing bang that echoed throughout the whole castle, and I heard the men behind us yell with shock and pain.

I ordered to Lucy to go and hide behind the wall in the middle of the ground floor, and I hid at the side of the archway entrance with my baton poised. As the noise of the footsteps became louder and closer, I crouched down, and as soon as the first man ran out, I swung my baton round smashing into his shins. I quickly stood up and sent a right upper cut to the man's chin, knocking him clean out. I could actually hear the crack of his jaw breaking as the knuckle duster made contact with his chin.

The other two men squeezed through the archway, and were both facing me. The henchman on my right was holding a baseball bat, and I ducked just in time as it came swinging towards my head. Unfortunately, I wasn't swift enough to avoid the other man's foot as it smacked into my head, knocking me over onto my back and I dropped the baton. The man with the baseball bat stood over me, and just as he lifted the bat above his head to strike. I rammed my right foot in between his legs. While he was doubled up in agony from having his testicles kicked up to where his Adam's apple was, I brought my foot back up again, connecting it with his head, and sent him flying onto his back. He was out cold.

The third thug jumped and I rolled onto my front to avoid him landing on my chest. He continued to stamp his feet trying to land on my chest, but I kept rolling out of his way. I could see the frustration building up in him as he kept missing with his foot. Immediately after his final effort, I spun around on my back, like a break dancer, swinging my right leg into the back of his. The momentum of my swinging legs hitting him sent him down onto his knees. I picked myself up and jumped onto his back, my body weight sending him to the floor. I sat over the small of his back and grabbed him by his throat, pulling his head upwards and restricting his breathing. The veins in his shaved head were bulging, almost to bursting point, and his face turned a beautiful shade of crimson. His struggling became weaker and he eventually passed out, and lay there in a dead heap.

As I picked myself up off the floor, the main entrance to the castle slammed shut, and when I turned I saw Eric standing there alongside two more of his hired muscle. Eric began giving me a slow sarcastic round of applause and was grinning from ear to ear.

"Very impressive," he said unconvincingly, "You really do have some fighting spirit."

I glanced over at Lucy and she remained behind the wall, cowering.

Eric walked down the steps from the main door towards me, leaving his two men standing guard at the entrance. He then glanced over at Lucy and said, "You've done well to get her past my lads, Mister Harrison. But I do hope that you realise that I am unable to allow you to leave here in one piece. Especially after your disrespectful actions against me and my business."

I laughed in disbelief. He actually thinks I'm being disrespectful for not allowing him to bully me. What was I supposed to do, just sit back and let him get on with it? His sheer audacity was beginning to piss me off.

"You know what?" I said, "You actually sometimes sound quite intelligent, considering you're a decrepit old twat who's made a living out of being nothing but a fucking thug. But now, these days, you haven't even got the bollocks to do it for yourself. You get docile young men who want to think they're something, and use them to do your dirty work. You're a fucking has been, Barnes, and your days are numbered!"

"Well it's been my intelligence that's got me where I am now?" Eric added.

"What?" I continued, "Stood in a dark dingy castle, fighting over a slack handful of paper? I think I've got you scared, haven't I? That paperwork I've got could ruin you if it was in the wrong hands, and you know it. You're shitting it, aren't you?"

Eric smiled as he reached into his jacket pocket, pulled out a pistol and pointed it at me. He had now crossed the line with me. I took a deep breathe and slowly walked towards him, until the barrel was touching my forehead. I stared straight into Eric's old grey eyes.

"You honestly think I'm scared of having one of those things pointed at me? I've seen and done things that would probably make you piss the bed and have nightmares, you old bastard. I've handled a lot worse than an old man and a bunch of thick headed cardboard gangsters."

Using his thumb, Eric pulled back the hammer on the pistol, and pressed the end of the barrel hard onto my forehead.

"You pull that trigger, old man, and you will go down. Not just for murder, but for every dodgy fucking thing you've ever done or involved in. You think I'm daft enough to have your paperwork in my pocket?" I said through gritted teeth.

"Then you're definitely not as intelligent as you make out, Mister Harrison," Eric snarled, "No paperwork, no deal. You've really disappointed me. And you really don't realise what you've let yourself in for."

"You weren't going to let me out of here anyway, were you?" I screamed, "Now if you're going to use that thing, I suggest you do it now!"

Eric slowly squeezed the trigger, and I could see the hammer twitch. I continued to stare into his eyes, and my breathe became uncontrollably heavy.

Suddenly, the castle entrance door swung open, knocking one of Eric's boys to the floor. It was Jez and Lurch. Eric jerked his head around to see what the commotion was, and I saw this as my opportunity to act fast. I grabbed hold of Eric's wrist with my left hand, and pulled downwards as my right hand grabbed the pistol barrel and pushed it upwards. This movement forced Eric to loose grip of the pistol, and I now had hold of it by the barrel.

Jez jumped onto the man he had knocked to the floor, and rained down onto his face with a barrage of fists. Lurch grabbed the other suited man by the face with one of his shovel like hands, and pushed him up against the castle wall. The force of his being shoved against the wall knocked him out, and he crumpled to the floor.

Holding onto the pistol barrel, I swung and hit Eric in the side of the head with the pistol's hand grip, sending him to the floor. I pressed the release button to allow the magazine to drop out, and then threw the pistol over to the far side of the castle.

Eric quickly reached into another of his pockets and pulled out a small knife. He lashed out and just caught my leg, cutting through my trousers and gashing my calf. I howled with anger, and I could feel a massive surge of fury take over me. My body oozed pure rage. I dropped down, sinking my knees onto his chest which winded him and probably broke a few ribs in the process.

Pinning down his arms with my knees, I straddled over him and laid into his face. His head rocked from side to side as my fists rained down on him. Blood and teeth splattered from his mouth, and he was rapidly losing consciousness. Out of the corner of my eye, I noticed the baseball bat from earlier, so I leaned over and grabbed it. With both hands wrapped around the handle, I raised the bat above my head, and just as I was about to bring it crashing down, Lurch's hand pulled it from my grip.

"Mark!" he screamed, "He's the murderer, mate. Not you!"

Lurch wrapped his arms around my chest, and pulled me away from Eric. I sat on the floor and looked at Eric's blood soaked face. The knuckle duster had made one hell of a mess. I remained sitting on the floor until I calmed down and eventually my breathing became manageable. My body began to shake as the adrenalin disappeared.

As I stood up, Lucy came running towards me and showered me with hugs and kisses. She was sobbing hysterically, and I wrapped my arms around her, telling her it was over, and that she would be okay. Lurch and Jez joined us, and I asked them to take Lucy to the castle entrance and wait for me.

I limped over to where Eric was lying, and gently tapped him on the side of the ribs with my left boot. He winced and moaned with pain, and I knelt down by his side and grabbed him by his jacket.

"Let this be a fucking warning, Barnes. You are nothing to me, and if you or any of your meat heads so much as breath in my air space, I will rip your fucking throat out. It's over, and your time is up. You understand?" I whispered to him through clenched teeth.

I left Eric lying in his blood, and walked over to Jez, Lurch and Lucy. Jez put his arm around my shoulder and we walked out of the castle.

"I've brought the car, mate," Jez said, "Thought you might

need a lift home."

We turned left in the castle grounds, headed off the gravel path, and headed down towards the park. There were a few metal rungs missing from the fence, so we squeezed through the gap and made our way to the car. Jez remotely opened his car as we neared it, and I opened the front passenger door and slumped into the seat. I was knackered. Once everyone was in the car, Jez started the engine and drove out of the car park. He turned right onto the main road, and began heading past the front of the castle grounds. As we approached the castle gates, I remembered something.

"Shit. Stop the car a minute, mate." I said to Jez.

Jez came to a halt and I jumped out the car. I ran over to the fence and climber over back into the castle grounds. I limped along the gravel pathway until I approached the old gravestone, and reached behind it.

As I got back into the car, Jez asked, "What the bloody hell was all that about?"

I waved a brown envelope in his face and replied, "You think I was going to walk right into Eric's little trap carrying his paperwork in my pocket? Ha! I'm not as daft as you look, you know."

"Jez laughed and commented, "You're a crafty twat, Mark, But a good one"

"Anyway," I changed the subject slightly, "What happened to waiting until midnight to call the police?"

Jez looked at me with a smile, "You think I was going to leave you all alone in there? Not only that, I wasn't letting you have *all* the fun."

Chapter 15

As soon as we arrived back home, I took Lucy upstairs and ran her a nice hot bath. I gave her one of my t shirts and a pair of shorts to change into, and my mother's dressing gown to cover her dignity. While Lucy was bathing, I went back downstairs to check on the boys. As I walked into the living room, Jez put his finger to his lips for me to remain silent and pointed at Nick. He was fast asleep on the couch, and Clive was also slumped on his chair snoring through his broken nose.

I crept over to Nick and crouched down so my face was level with his.

"Oi!" I shouted.

Nick almost jumped out of his skin, and Jez and Lurch were crying with laughter.

"Jesus Christ, man!" Nick moaned, "I think I've just shit my pants."

I patted him on the shoulder and asked if everything was okay.

"Oh, aye," he replied, "Dumb fuck over there has been sleeping, so I got my head down for a bit."

"Nice one," I said, "Right, well we need to get rid of Clivey boy, before people start snooping, and then we need to get cleaned up."

"What we going to do with him, mate?" Jez asked.

"Oh we'll just dump him in the car and take him home. I'll have a little chat with him first though." I replied.

The loud, rude awakening I gave Nick had also woken up Clive, and his eyes followed me as I walked to his front.

"See this?" I asked as I put my hands up in front of his face. "It's Eric's blood, not mine. And the fact that I'm stood here talking to you will let you know that I fucking won. Don't you think?"

Clive nodded nervously.

"Don't worry," I continued, "I haven't killed him. Well I don't think I have anyway. His days as a big time thug are over, which means that you are fucking unemployed. Now, we're going to take you home in a bit, so if you ever open your gob to anyone about what's happened, I'll be coming for you. And next time, I'll do more than tie you up and rip your fucking eyebrows off. You understand?"

Clive nodded again.

I wasn't finished, "When we take you home, get yourself cleaned up and then get yourself to the walk in centre to get checked over. And remember, don't say a fucking word, otherwise you'll be going swimming in the river wearing concrete socks."

On our way to Clive's home, I asked Jez if he could take a quick detour past the castle at Hylton Dene. When we passed the grounds, the main gates were wide open, and I could see three police cars and a van with their blue lights flashing in the grounds. Police were running towards the castle.

"That'll be Eric fucked now." I said triumphantly.

"I fucking hope so mate. I can't handle this shit on a regular basis. My head will end up just as mashed up as yours." Jez laughed.

"Well I'm not finished yet Jez." I said, "Could you stop off by a post box on the way? I've got something urgent to deliver."

We drove into Castletown, and when we neared the old post office, Jez stopped the car directly next to the post box. I got out the car and dropped the brown envelope into it.

"So who've you posted that to, mate?" Jez asked as I got

back into the car.

"Oh, I've just sent some information to the police station. Think they might be interested in the paperwork I found belonging to Eric. I've put a little note in there too, just to explain what it's all about." I replied.

I turned to face Clive in the back seat and smirked, "You're little world's about to coming crashing down, sunshine. Suppose you'll have to find another job now, and actually work for a living. That's if you don't end up doing a bit of time inside."

We drove down Jennifer Avenue and stopped outside Clive's house. Before I let him out, I gave him a little reminder.

"Right, fuck face. Let's make sure that this is the last time I ever have to come to your house. Remember to keep that mouth of yours shut for once. Now fuck off!"

Clive got out the car, and without even looking back, he opened the front door and slammed it behind him as he went in.

Jez turned his car around and we made our way back home. We were welcomed back into the house with hot cups of coffee and a huge stack of bacon sandwiches. Lucy had sorted herself out, but still looked understandably haggard.

The five of us sat around the table, and we tucked into the sandwiches. Not a lot was said while we ate, but I kept an eye on Lucy, giving her the occasional smile to reassure her.

"Right lads," I said, "Thank you for everything you've all done. I owe you all big time."

"Fucking right you do!" Jez said, laughing.

"Well I think we should lay low for a few days until things cool off a bit. I haven't got a clue how this is going to pan out, so just keep your heads down until I know what's going on." I said.

"So what do we do if it all kicks off? What if the coppers turn up?" Nick asked.

"The best thing to do right now," I replied, "If you lot get yourselves back home and just stay out of the way for a few days or so. If the coppers come and ask you anything, just plead ignorance and say you haven't seen me for days. Leave the rest to me. Then once this has all blown over, we're going to have the mother of all piss ups, on me!"

I then turned to Lucy and said, "Lucy, sweetheart, if it's okay with you, I'd like you to stay here for a couple of days. You can ring your family and just say your staying at your friend's place or something. I just want to make sure you're okay."

An hour or so later, the boys made their way back to their own homes, and I sorted out my mother's room for Lucy to use. She was absolutely exhausted, and still a bit shaken, so she went straight to bed. I went into the kitchen and grabbed a black bin liner from under the sink, then ran upstairs and stripped naked in my room. Everything went into the bin bag, including the contents of my pockets. I then went into the shower and scrubbed myself from head to foot. My whole body was aching, and I felt totally exhausted. I watched the blood wash away from me and drain into the bath plug hole. The heat of the water made my body tingle, but it was a pleasant feeling that relaxed me.

After drying myself off, and covering the superficial cut on my calf, I put on a pair of shorts. I peered into my mother's room to check on Lucy, and she was sleeping peacefully. Slowly and quietly, I closed the bedroom door and made my way back into my room. I lay on top of my bed and tried going to sleep, but my head was still buzzing over what had happened tonight.

It had taken me a long time to drift off, and the last time I remembered looking at the alarm clock, it was almost half past seven.

I must've been asleep for only three hours or so, when I heard a loud knock at the door. I crept downstairs in the hope that the knocking hadn't woke up Lucy, and then answered the door. As I was in shorts, I stood behind the door to hide my modesty, and peered my head around to see two policemen waiting.

"Mister Harrison?" One of the policemen asked.

"Yep, that's me. How can I help?" I replied.

Could you tell us where you were between the hours of ten o'clock last night and one o'clock this morning?" he asked.

Just as I was about to answer, Lucy stood at the top of the stairs, wearing nothing but my t shirt, and shouted down.

"Erm, excuse me Mark, but get your sexy arse back up these stairs, we're not finished yet. Five times in one night ain't good enough for me, sweetheart."

I looked up the stairs to Lucy, gave her a wink and shouted back, "No probs darling, I won't be long."

The two policemen were smiling when I turned back to look at them, and I asked, "Sorry about that. What did you say?"

"Erm," the policeman stuttered, "I asked if you could account for your whereabouts last night."

"Ha!" I laughed, "Well you're the copper, mate. I'm sure you can work out what I've been busy doing all night. Now if you don't mind, I've got some unfinished business to sort out upstairs, if you know what I mean."

"Okay then, Mister Harrison. We won't bother you again." The policeman said.

"Anyway. What you asking me that for? What's going on?" I asked, just as they were leaving.

"Oh, we're just making enquiries regarding on incident at Hylton Dene last night. It's nothing for you to worry about. Have a good day." He replied as they both turned and walked away.

I closed the door, and laughed to myself as I walked upstairs. Lucy was waiting at the top leaning against my mother's bedroom door.

"Now you're a naughty girl, aren't you?" I said, still laughing.

"You must be rubbing off on me. I used to be a good girl, you know." she replied.

We both stood facing each other for a few quiet moments, and I stared into her eyes. Although I knew that she would never forget what had happened, I could see that the fear had gone from her eyes. I wrapped my arms around her and gave her a kiss on her forehead.

"Everything's going to be okay, Lucy." I said to her, "It's all over now, and I'm so sorry that you've been dragged into something that you had nothing to do with. I will not let anyone harm you again, okay?"

Lucy gave me a little peck on my lips and replied, "You've got nothing to be sorry for, Mark. You're a great bloke, and you've done nothing wrong. You just stood up for yourself, and you refused to take any crap."

"Right," I said as I gave her a final hug, "Make yourself decent and come downstairs. I'll get the kettle on."

I walked to the top of the stairs, and before I walked down, I stopped and turned to Lucy.

"Five times a nigh not good enough for you? You must eat your poor lad alive when he gets home." I said.

"Ha!" she laughed, "Oh aye, I'm an animal. In fact, if you were a few years younger...."

"Hey!" I interrupted, "No flirting with the boss, young lady. Get dressed, and then get your arse downstairs."

Lucy gave me a cheeky little wink, and as she walked back into my mother's room she said, "Okay tiger. I won't be long."

Lucy went back home after spending two days at my house. There were no more visits from the police, and the boys had contacted me to say that they hadn't heard anything or had any visits either. Despite this, I decided to lay low for a little longer, just to be on the safe side. My mother was due back with Aunt Linda and Cameron in a few days, so I thought it would be a good idea if I gave the house a good spring clean.

I scrubbed the house from top to bottom until it was practically clinically clean. I put the bin bag filled with my combats into the bottom of the wheelie bin out in the back garden. That was due to be emptied in a couple of days, so that would deal with getting rid of any incriminating evidence, before it fell into the wrong hands.

I rang the local florists and ordered a couple of bunches of flowers, and had them delivered so I didn't have to eave the house. I placed one bunch in the middle of the dining table, and the other on the hearth. I wasn't personally into flowers, but my mother loves them. The fragrance also came in handy with ridding the smell of Clive's blood and sweaty carcass.

Just as I was about to relax on the sofa, there was a knock at the front door, but before I could get up to answer it, I heard the familiar welcome call from Jez. He waltzed into the living room with a huge cheesy grin on his face, and he threw a newspaper onto my lap.

"Get a load of the front page, mate. It'll make you smile." he said smugly.

I unravelled the newspaper and read the front page headline, and it certainly did put a smile on my face - *"Veteran Hard Man in Custody"*.

I went over to the dining table where Jez was sat, and placed the newspaper in front of me.

"So, what's happening then?" I asked.

Jez pushed the paper closer to me and replied, "Well read it then, daft arse. I'm not going to spoil it for you. I'll get the kettle on."

Jez stood up and walked into the kitchen as I began to read the story.

"Just days after being found badly beaten in what appeared to be a gang related incident, old time hard man, Eric Barnes has been arrested after receiving an anonymous tip off.

A police spokesman confirmed that information had been received, resulting in searches carried out at Barnes's Hylton Castle office and home, and his subsequent arrest.

Weapons were found during the search, along with an

undisclosed amount of cash. Information had also been discovered to connect Eric Barnes with illegal money lending and the running of protection rackets. It is believed that many small businesses and local shops have been forced into paying money to "Epic Security Company" in exchange for not being threatened.

Police are urging anyone who has fallen victim to these crimes to step forward and give any information they possibly can. Police are also asking for information regarding the Hylton Dene incident."

The grin on my face couldn't get any bigger, even if I tried, and Jez was also still smiling when he came through from the kitchen.

"Looks like a result, eh?" Jez said as he handed me a cup of coffee.

"Oh yes, indeedy," I said, "I've got a feeling that we're not going to see Eric and his boys for a very long time. Especially if anyone has the balls to come forward to give evidence."

Jez sat at the table, took a sip from his coffee and said, "Well, it's about fucking time he got what he deserves."

Chapter 16

Nick, Lurch and Jez were good enough to come round to my house to welcome back my mother, Aunt Linda and Cameron. We knew that as soon as they arrive, mum and Aunt Linda would demand a cup of tea, so the cups were charged up, ready to go in the kitchen. I also bought a pack of mum's favourite fruit scones.

We were sat in the living room when the front door opened, and I stood up to wait for them coming in. When they walked into the room, mum let Cameron toddle straight over to me. I crouched down with my arms outstretched in front of me, and Cameron gave me a huge hug as I wrapped my arms around him and picked him up.

"Be a love, Jeremy, and get the cases from outside please. The taxi driver's just unloading them now." Mum asked Jez.

As Jez stood up, he gave Nick a nudge and asked him to help him bring the cases in, so they both left to grab the luggage.

Mum then turned to Lurch and said, "You know what I'm going to ask you, don't you, sweetheart?"

"The cups are already loaded up and waiting, Margie," Lurch replied as he stood up, "I'll just go and boil the kettle."

Aunt Linda slumped onto the sofa and kicked off her sandals. Giving out a huge sigh of relief. My mother came over to me and hugged me, while I was still holding on to Cameron.

"Everything okay, son?" she asked.

"Oh yes." I said, "It's been an eventful week, but me and lads have got it all sorted."

Mum frowned as she asked, "Why don't I like the sound of

that? What do you mean by being eventful?"

I looked over to the dining table where I had left the newspaper and replied, "Just have a read of that, mam. Let's just say that we shouldn't be seeing Eric Barnes around for a while."

Aunt Linda got up and followed my mother over to the table and they both leaned over to read it together. I could see the smile getting bigger and bigger on my mother's face.

"Erm, I won't bother asking about how he managed to get beaten up in Hylton Dene." she commented.

"Aye, mam," I said, "The less you know the better."

Jez and Nick had left the luggage in the hallway, and just as they were sitting down, Lurch came in carrying two cups of tea for my mother and Aunt Linda.

"There you go ladies. Sit down and enjoy." He said to them as he handed the cups over.

"So where's our cuppas, like?" Nick asked.

"You know where the kitchen is, cheeky twat." Lurch cursed.

"Now, now, let's keep the language down. There's a child and ladies present." Aunt Linda ordered.

"Nick laughed and joked, "Well I can see the bairn, but where's the ladies."

Lurch turned his back to hide his laugh, and I just burst into tears with laughter, as Aunt Linda stood back up and clipped Nick across the back of the head.

The joviality was soon interrupted by the telephone ringing, so I walked into the hallway and answered the call.

Everyone noticed the numb look on my face when I walked back into the living room.

"What's up son? Who was that?" mum asked.

"That was the police on the phone." I replied, "They want me to go down to the station and give a statement. They're pinning Sandra's death on Eric."

When I arrived at the station, PC Lomas was already waiting for me at the reception. He escorted me into an interview room, and wrote down the details of my version of events regarding Sandra's death.

Once the statement was completed, PC Lomas gave it to me to check over and sign.

"So, what's going on then?" I asked as I handed back the statement.

"Well, Mister Harrison," he replied, "We have been informed by a reliable source that Eric Barnes was, in some way or another, involved in the death of your wife. I'm afraid that's all I can tell you for now, but no doubt you will hear more through the grapevine, or in the papers. Either way, it's not looking good for Eric Barnes."

"Let's hope they throw away the bloody key then!" I added as I got up to leave.

Just as PC Lomas predicted, three days after giving my statement, Sandra's death had made the front page of the local paper. In addition to the charges already made against him, Eric was now facing conspiracy to murder, as he had ordered one of his employees to tamper with Sandra's brakes. The employee had admitted to snipping the brake pipes, and has been charged with murder. My chin almost dropped to the floor when I read that the accused employee was Clive. Sandra had been killed by her own boyfriend!

As well as Eric and Clive, four others were remanded in custody awaiting trial. Between the six of them, there were charges of murder, conspiracy to murder, money laundering, protection racketeering, illegal money lending and tax evasion. The crooked empire of Eric Barnes had come to an almighty and sudden end.

Chapter 17

Despite me being away from The Sweat Box for well over a week, the customers were eager to get back to the fitness classes once I had reopened. I had contacted Lucy to see if she was okay coming back to work, and she was just as keen as me to get back to some sort of normality. We both spent a few days advertising and contacting existing customers, and within a week our schedule was booked up to the hilt. Even Nick and Lurch had started coming to some of them.

I had totally redecorated the unit, changing the colours from black and olive to red, yellow and blue. These are the colours of the Royal Electrical and Mechanical Engineers. The corridor was now plastered in some of my personal memorabilia from when I was in the army, and I spent a small fortune on camouflage nets to hang from the ceiling in the workout area.

As promised, I took Nick, Lurch, Jez and Lucy out for a night to remember. As we went from pub to pub, we noticed that all the doormen were fresh faces, obviously not from Epic Security. After a bit of snooping around and a few chats with the new doormen, I found out that Epic Security Company had gone into administration, and all of his security men had their SIA licences revoked. This made our night out that little bit more special.

The alcohol flowed heavily all night, and my head certainly let me know about it the next morning when I eventually dragged myself out of bed. My whole body was aching, and my stomach was churning almost to the point of vomiting. After peeling my tongue from the roof of my mouth, I forced a cup of coffee down me in the hope that it would sober me up a little. Not a chance!

Thankfully, my mother had already been up with Cameron and they had gone out for the day, so I decided to spend some time on the sofa, feeling sorry for myself while it was peaceful.

I heard mail being pushed through the letterbox, so I dragged myself off the sofa and shuffled into the hallway to collect it from the doorstep. One of the letters was addressed to me, and it looked official. I threw the rest of the mail onto the dining table, and then sank back onto the sofa with my letter.

The letter was from a counselling service in Newcastle, stating that the army had requested that I attend some regular sessions in order to get to the bottom of some "issues" of mine. I suppose I had nothing to lose and it wouldn't do me any harm by paying them a few visits, so I picked up the telephone to arrange my first meeting.

My appointment was nothing like I was expecting. I imagined lying on a leather sofa talking about my life, while a psychiatrist sat behind me taking notes. The counsellor took me into a small well lit room that looked like a basic living room. There were two leather sofas, a small flat screen television and a few random floral pictures scattered around the room to make the place appear more homely.

We started off by Sheila, my counsellor, explaining what we were going to do. She wanted to start from the very beginning, so she asked a lot of probing questions about my childhood and my upbringing. Although I found this irrelevant, I answered everything.

I then went on, briefly, about my army background, telling her about where I had been and what I had experienced, including the court martial.

Considering Sheila was supposed to be giving me the counselling, I did the majority of the talking. She would ask the occasional question, and then I would babble on for minutes on end. She wasn't even taking any notes.

"Do you miss the army?" Sheila asked.

"I miss it loads, and at times, I wish I was back with them all. But at the same time, I've had my eyes opened, and glad I'm away."

"And why are you glad you're away?" She asked more.

"Because of the court martial" I replied, "I was treat like shit. It was if the army had said *thanks for your service Sergeant Harrison, now fuck off!*"

"So what do you think of the army now then, Mark?" Sheila asked after a short pause.

"Well, I don't hate it," I continued, "I just hate the way I was treated near the end. In general, I fucking love the army, because it made me feel like I belonged."

The questions got deeper and deeper, and we eventually came to the initial conclusion that I had been institutionalised. The army discipline had been drummed into me, and despite the positive effects it's had on me, the difficulty of letting go of this way of thinking and the army way of life was the result of me struggling to settle back into civilian life.

I was, apparently, only entitled to eight one hour sessions, but after attending my initial appointment, Sheila already knew that it would take longer to help me. Once the first session was over, I did actually feel slightly relieved, and felt like a huge weight had been lifted from my shoulders. Years ago, I would not have dreamed of doing anything like this. I would quite often, take the piss out of people such as counsellors, calling them "tree huggers". But now I can say I've had my opinions changed. I was just going to take time to adjust.

Chapter 18

I dropped Cameron off at the nursery, and then walked around to the newsagents for a paper. Since the incident with Eric Barnes, I liked to keep myself up to date on his case, and see what the latest gossip was in the media.

Once again, Eric had made the front page. The judge had sentenced him to eighteen years for a total of four charges, including conspiracy to murder. Apparently, he had been lucky that no one came forward with any more damning evidence; otherwise he had probably died behind bars. But, there was enough evidence gathered to justify the sentence he was given.

Clive was sentenced to life for the murder of Sandra, and apparently, he had pathetically pleaded that he was forced into doing the deed. Unfortunately for him, his plea fell on deaf ears and the judge threw the book at him.

Eric's reign had come to an end, and Epic Security was no more. All of Eric's assets, including his home had been seized as it was proved that they were bought from the proceeds of his crimes.

None of the stories in the papers about Eric had ever mentioned what had actually happened that night at Hylton Dene. Apparently, he was involved in an "altercation" with a rival gang. But no names were ever mentioned, and no other arrests were ever made outside of Eric's gang. It was over for me, I'm in the clear.

Over a matter of a few weeks, I had attended quite a few sessions with Sheila, and I was slowly but surely feeling a lot better within myself. I had a long way to go, but I was getting there.

Despite my attitude towards civilian society, I was gradually learning to control my thoughts and keep them to myself. The ignorance of others still boiled my piss, but that was their problem, not mine. And I was doing well not to take me anger out on them. Sheila had shown me a few relaxation techniques that came in handy whenever I felt like I was about to "explode", but I still relied on my punch bag for the occasional release of aggression.

Although I felt that my army career and my life had been robbed from me, I now understand that I should not have let my emotions get the better of me. I was a professional soldier at the time, and I should've been able to control myself more.

I've started to learn how to be more positive with myself and others, and to concentrate on the future, rather than pondering on the past. There was nothing I could do to change the past, so I might as well get on with it. I had witnessed some terrible things in my time, and they have affected me in some form or another, and although I would never forget, I had to put those memories behind me somewhere.

Regardless of what I have witnessed, and regardless of what I have lost and been through, I just keep thinking that I still have a lot going for me, and there's a lot of people out there a lot worse off than me. I've got my family and friends around me, and my life is now more than comfortable. I have my own business with plenty of money coming in which keeps me and my family well above water.

All of this aside, there is one thing that I will say though. You might be able to take the soldier out of the army, but you will never take the army out of the soldier............

Printed in Great Britain
by Amazon.co.uk, Ltd.,
Marston Gate.